THE **G**LOBE **R**EADER'S **C**OLLECTION

P9-BIT-351

MYTHS AND STORIES FROM THE AMERICAS

GLOBE FEARON EDUCATIONAL PUBLISHER
A Division of Simon & Schuster
Upper Saddle River, New Jersey

Executive Editor: Barbara Levadi
Senior Editor: Bernice Golden
Editors: Helene Avraham, Laura Baselice, Robert McIlwaine
Product Development: PubWorks, Inc.
Production Manager: Penny Gibson
Senior Production Editor: Linda Greenberg
Production Editor: Walt Niedner
Marketing Manager: Sandra Hutchison
Electronic Page Production: The Wheetley Company, Inc.
Cover Design: The Wheetley Company, Inc.
Cover Art: Montas Antoine's *Goat Herd* Van Hoorick, SuperStock, Inc.
Illustrator: Larry Frederick

Printed in the United States of America
1 2 3 4 5 6 7 8 9 10 99 98 97 96 95

ISBN: 0-8359-1368-6

GLOBE FEARON EDUCATIONAL PUBLISHER
A Division of Simon & Schuster
Upper Saddle River, New Jersey

TABLE OF CONTENTS

READING STORIES FROM THE AMERICAS   **1**

Stories from North America and Hawaii

SCARFACE a story from the Blackfoot   **6**
adapted from the translation by George Bird Grinnell
> A poor young man with a scarred face goes on a quest
> for permission to marry a beautiful woman. In the
> end, he wins much more than a bride.

THE DAY IT SNOWED TORTILLAS   **17**
a Spanish folktale from New Mexico by Joe Hayes
> It's not enough to have the luck to find three bags of
> gold beside the road. You also have to know how to
> hold on to your good fortune.

THE CRADLE DIDN'T ROCK   **24**
an African American tale retold by Julius Lester
> Brer Rabbit cleverly traps Brer Wolf into believing that
> Mr. Man has a gift for him.

OJEEG, THE HUNTER, AND THE ICE MAN   **31**
from the Micmac of Canada retold by Dorothy de Wit
> The hunter Ojeeg, his son, and a sympathetic squirrel
> agree—winter sticks around too long. But it's not easy
> to get rid of the old Ice Man.

THE MAIZE SPIRIT a Chippewa tale   **40**
retold by Lewis Spence
> A Chippewa teenager fasts for days and engages in
> combat as his rite of passage into manhood. He not
> only succeeds, but also prevents the starvation of his
> people.

WHY CORN HAS SILKY WHITE HAIR   **47**
a Southern United States tale retold by Anne Pellowski
> Being friendly and clever can get results almost any-
> where. According to this story from the South, it can
> even delay death.

GINGER FOR THE HEART   54
a story of Chinese immigrants in the New World
by Paul Yee

> Chinese traditions, thousands of years old, sustain love
> and hope in a new land. Love burns in the heart as gin-
> ger does on the tongue.

HOW THUNDER AND LIGHTNING   62
CAME TO BE an Eskimo myth
by Ramona Maher

> Two Eskimo children are left home alone. The results
> are stormy indeed!

A STRANGE SLED RACE a Hawaiian myth   71
by Vivian L. Thompson

> Two goddesses compete against each other in a spec-
> tacular sled race on the island of Hawaii. It turns out
> that they're playing for keeps.

Stories from the Caribbean

ATARIBA AND NIGUAYONA   79
a legend from the Taino People of Puerto Rico
adapted by Harriet Rohmer and Jesús Guerrero Rea

> A boy searches the jungle for the cure for a mysterious
> disease. A friendly fruit leads the way.

PEDRO ANIMALA AND THE CARRAO BIRD   86
a Puerto Rican folktale by Pura Belpré

> It's usually no fun to be tricked by someone. In this
> story, the trick does no harm, and everybody enjoys the
> joke. Well . . . maybe everybody.

A VERY HAPPY DONKEY a Haitian folktale   93
retold by Diane Wolkstein

> People are often outsmarted by clever foxes, wise owls,
> and sneaky snakes. It takes someone pretty special,
> though, to be outsmarted by a donkey.

THE LITTLE GREEN FROG   100
a tale from the Dominican Republic
translated by Mary Hanson

On a fine day in the Dominican Republic, a a girl finds
a frog. Amazingly, the frog talks. . . and tells a sad,
ancient tale ending in modern injustice.

Stories from Central America

DOOMED LOVERS an Aztec tale   111
retold by Ben Sonder

The deep love of a powerful Aztec warrior and a loyal
Aztec princess for one another reaches new heights.
Monuments to their love tower above Mexico City even
today.

SEÑOR COYOTE AND THE TRICKED   121
TRICKSTER a Mexican folktale
by I.G. Edmonds

Read about a meeting of three tricky minds in Mexico.
A mouse, a coyote, and a snake all outsmart one
another.

THE STORY OF THE LAZY MAN WHO   130
GOT TO BE KING OF A TOWN
a Mayan folktale from Guatemala
by Ignacio Bizarro Ujpán
translated and edited by James D. Sexton

Hard work is not the only way to succeed. Sometimes,
it's not what you know, but whom you know that
makes the difference.

THE BOW, THE DEER, AND THE   140
TALKING BIRD a Mexican folktale
retold by Anita Brenner

How does the youngest son of an Aztec merchant
become the prime minister to the king? Perhaps it's
something a little bird told him.

LORD SUN'S BRIDE a Mayan tale   **148**
edited by John Bierhorst

> Lord Sun takes a shine to a beautiful young woman
> and decides he wants to marry her. She rises to the
> occasion.

Stories from South America

THE BAKER'S NEIGHBOR a story from Peru   **157**
translated by Frank Henius and adapted by Ben Sonder

> The best things in life are free. Or are they? A baker
> seeks to charge for the scents from his oven.

THE GREEN MOSS PRINCE a story from Uruguay **167**
translated by Frank Henius

> Beautiful Florinda loves a parrot prince, who loves her.
> Then, she is betrayed by false friends, and her parrot
> prince puts her love to the test.

DON'T MAKE A BARGAIN WITH A FOX   **180**
a folktale from Argentina
by M. A. Jagendorf and R. S. Boggs

> When a fox does you a favor, you must beware. You
> will probably pay for it one way or another.

THE TREE OF LIFE a story of the Carib People   **187**
retold by Richard Alan Young and Judy Dockrey Young

> The Carib people and their animal friends live for
> many years without much to eat. Then, a little detec-
> tive work uncovers a bonanza.

HOW THE ALLIGATOR GOT HIS SCALES   **195**
a tale from the Amazon by Elsie Spicer Fields

> The God Rairu wants to control his favorite creatures,
> the rose and silver fish. An alligator sticks his snout
> into the business and then takes his lumps.

ACKNOWLEDGMENTS   **202**

READING STORIES FROM THE AMERICAS

The stories in this book come from many cultures in the Americas. Most of them show, in some way, the special qualities and characteristics of a culture. The stories also reveal how basic human emotions—love, hate, jealousy, generosity, laziness—are universal and can appear in the cultures of all people.

The categories of myth, folktale, and legend overlap in some ways, but there are significant differences among them. Myths are usually cultural explanations for natural happenings, major historical events, or religious beliefs, and often involve gods and goddesses. Many of the myths in this book provide explanations for such things as sunshine, lightning and thunder, for which we have scientific explanations today.

A folktale is a story that was first told aloud over and over again for many years before it was written. Characters in folktales, unlike those in most short stories, usually show only one personality trait. The character, which is often an animal, may be strong, smart, stupid, or beautiful. This quality is exaggerated in a folktale. Also, characters with attractive qualities, such as beauty and intelligence, are rewarded. Bad or foolish characters are usually punished. The Brer Rabbit stories of the U.S. South present a whole group of these characters. Brer Rabbit is clever, Brer Bear is stupid, and Brer Wolf is bad. Generally, folktales are funny.

A legend is a story, also told aloud at first, about a character who actually lived or an event that actually happened. As the story was told over and over, the details became more and more elaborate and the characters more and more extraordinary. Some legendary characters eventually become almost superhuman. A good example is Hiawatha, the legendary Onondaga chief, who united the Iroquois people. It is likely that Hiawatha did this around the year 1450. His legend has made him a central figure of Native American culture. He represents human progress and civilization. Hiawatha is a legend not only for Native Americans but for all Americans.

The stories in this volume come from the four major areas of the Americas: North America, the Caribbean, Central America, and South America. The stories have been chosen to reflect the wide cultural diversity of the Americas. Stories with Native American origins have been chosen over stories with European origins. This approach adds to stories in standard anthologies, which might include stories mostly by and about U.S. citizens of European background.

Often, a story passes from an ancient people through a more recent culture. "Doomed Lovers," a story about the mythical origins of the volcanoes, Popacatepetl and Ixtacihuatl, is thought to date back to the Maya, who lived in Mexico as early as the year 250. The version in this volume is from the Aztecs, who conquered Mexico around the year 1200. "Señor Coyote and the Tricked Trickster" is a story that appears in several Native American cultures. The version you will read has been retold by Mexican Latinos.

You will notice that geographic differences affect the content of the stories. We meet animals in South America, never seen farther north, such as the *viscacha*, a creature that looks like a rabbit but has a tail like a rat. The vegetation and terrain also affect the stories. The details in "The Little Green Frog" show us a setting in a lush rain forest of the past. The story also shows us the modern destruction of this tropical paradise.

Stories from North America and Hawaii

Half of the stories in this unit are Native American. Each story highlights some important aspect of Native

American storytelling. "Scarface" is a quest story. The main character must go on a long and dangerous journey to achieve his goal. In "Scarface," the hero achieves much more than he intends. "The Maize Spirit" tells of a young man's initiation into manhood, a theme that runs through the stories of all native peoples. "How Thunder and Lightning Came to Be" and "Ojeeg, the Hunter, and the Ice Man" are creation stories. "The Day It Snowed Tortillas," from Spanish New Mexico, is in the tradition of Latino stories of the clever, resourceful wife who knows much more than how to keep house. "Why the Corn Has Silky White Hair" and "The Cradle Didn't Rock," stories from the southern United States, are written in dialect, the natural speech of the characters. The latter story introduces the "trickster," a type of character popular in stories everywhere. He tricks others for his own profit—and for the pure fun of it. "Ginger for the Heart" provides a view of how the ancient culture of China is both honored and changed in a new land. True love and dedication triumph. "A Strange Sled Race" is from Hawaii.

Stories from the Caribbean

"Atariba and Niguayona," a story of the native Taino people of Puerto Rico, is similar to "Scarface" in the North American section. A young man goes on a quest for a specific purpose, to acquire some medicine, and gains much more. "Pedro Animala and the Carrao Bird" introduces us to another trickster, a legendary figure in Puerto Rico whose thinking is always several steps ahead of his victims. "A Very Happy Donkey," from Haiti, tells the story of a well-meaning boy whose thinking is several steps behind his donkey's. "The Little Green Frog" is a story within a story. The reader is suddenly taken from the modern world to an enchanted world of long ago and then back to the present.

Stories from Central America

"Doomed Lovers," an Aztec story, tells of a love as complete as that in "Ginger for the Heart" in Unit 1, but the ending is tragic. In "Señor Coyote and the Tricked Trickster," we meet a south-of-the-border trickster whose victims are as smart as he is. "The Story of the Lazy Man Who Got to Be King of a Town" is the first of three stories with strong supernatural forces. The lazy man finds help in the spirit world. A young man finds fame and fortune with the help of a bird in "The Bow, the Deer, and the Talking Bird." And the sun itself becomes a bumbling trickster in "Lord Sun's Bride."

Stories from South America

"The Baker's Neighbor" is in the European tradition of stories about the Seven Deadly Sins. In this case, the sinner is a greedy baker. The heroine of "The Green Moss Prince" must prove her love in a trial of endurance and dedication. We meet another trickster of the Argentine pampas in "Don't Make a Bargain with a Fox." The last two stories come from the Carib people of northern South America. "The Tree of Life" is a creation myth about the plentiful food of the region. The title "How the Alligator Got His Scales" gives away the plot, but this simple myth is particularly reminiscent of many myths: There is an all-powerful god who prefers some creatures to others, and there is a reptile who knows too much. The diversity of these selections is in their settings and expressions of cultural belief and custom. The motives and actions of the characters have much in common. Even the fantastic transformation and strange plot of "The Green Moss Prince" will seem believable to you in the context of pure, unfailing love.

Unit 1
STORIES FROM NORTH AMERICA AND HAWAII

SCARFACE
a story from the Blackfoot
Adapted from the translation by George Bird Grinnell

One of the earliest collectors of Native American stories in the United States was George Bird Grinnell. Unlike most people in the United States in the late 1800s and early 1900s, Grinnell admired Native American cultures. He was particularly interested in the customs of the Pawnee, Blackfoot, and Cheyenne nations. In order to gain a real understanding of these people, he spent many years getting to know them and living with them.

In 1892, Grinnell's book, Blackfoot Lodge Tales, *was published. It combines a history of the Blackfoot with a collection of their stories. He presents the stories as they were told to him. Thus, he provides an accurate portrayal of the Blackfoot way of life. The story that follows explains the origin of the Medicine Lodge.*

VOCABULARY WORDS

tanned (TAND) treated (animal hide) to turn it into leather
❖ The *tanned* deer hide was used to make a pair of moccasins.

relations (rih-LAY-shuhnz) relatives
❖ He went to the family reunion because he hadn't seen his *relations* in ten years.

designing (dih-ZYN-ihng) plotting; scheming
❖ The mystery was about a *designing* man who couldn't be trusted.

heeds (HEEDZ) pays careful attention to
❖ She *heeds* her grandmother's advice because she believes her to be a wise woman.

pemmican (PEHM-ih-kan) a paste of lean meat, fat, and other ingredients pounded into a paste
❖ *Pemmican* is a high-energy food.

bluffs (BLUFS) high, steep banks or cliffs
❖ We climbed the *bluffs* and had a grand view of the valley.

waded (WAYD-ihd) walked through water
❖ The child *waded* only a few feet into the lake because he didn't know how to swim.

sacred (SAY-krihd) holy; religious
❖ They bowed their heads and said the *sacred* words.

KEY WORDS

lodge (LAHDG) a building, often made of earth, used by Native Americans as a dwelling or for ceremonies.
❖ The *lodge* was used for honoring the rain god.

Medicine Lodge (MED-ih-sin LAHDG) a ceremonial lodge built for physical and spiritual well-being.
❖ The Blackfoot built their *Medicine Lodge* during the summer months.

 **I**n the earliest times, there was no war. All the tribes were at peace. In those days, there was a man who had a daughter, a very beautiful girl. Many young men wanted to marry her, but every time she was asked, she only shook her head and said she did not want a husband.

"How is this?" asked her father. "Some of these young men are rich, handsome, and brave."

"Why should I marry?" replied the girl. "I have a rich father and mother, and our lodge is good. There is always enough food, and there are plenty of tanned robes and soft furs for winter. But now hear the truth. That Above Person, the Sun, told me, 'Do not marry any of those men, for you are mine. You shall be happy and live to a great age.' Again he said, 'Take heed, you must not marry because you are mine.'"

Her father replied, "It must always be as he says." And they talked no more about it.

In the tribe, there was a very poor young man. His father, mother, and all his relations had gone to the Sand Hills (the afterlife), and he had no lodge and no wife to tan his robes or sew his moccasins. He would stop in one lodge for a day, and the next day he would eat and sleep in another. He was a good-looking young man, except that on his cheek he had a scar. His clothes were always old and poor.

One day Scarface went down by the river to wait where the women came to get water, and by and by the beautiful girl came along. He said, "Wait, I want to speak with you. Not as a designing person do I ask you, but openly where the Sun looks down and all may see."

"Speak then," said the girl.

"I have been watching," continued the young man. "You refuse those who are young, rich, and brave. Now, today, they laughed and said to me, 'Why do you not ask her?' I am poor, very poor. I have no lodge, no food, no clothes, no robes and warm furs. All my relations have gone to the Sand Hills. Yet, now, today, I ask you, take pity, be my wife."

The girl hid her face in her robe and brushed the ground with the point of her moccasin, back and forth, back and forth, for she was thinking. After a time she said, "True, I have refused all those rich young men. Now the poor one asks me, and I am glad. I will be your wife, and my people will be happy. You are poor, but it does not matter. My father will give you dogs, and my mother will make us a lodge. My people will give us robes and furs, and you will be poor no longer."

Then the young man was happy, and he started to kiss her. The girl held him back, however, and said, "Wait. The Sun has spoken to me, and he says I may not marry because I belong to him. He says if I listen to him, I shall live to a great age. So now, I ask you to go to the Sun and tell him: 'She whom you spoke with heeds your words. She has never done wrong, but now she wants to marry. I want her for my wife.' Ask him to take that scar from your face. That will be his sign that he is pleased. But if he refuses, or if you fail to find his lodge, then do not return to me."

Scarface was very sad, and he sat down and covered his head with his robe and tried to think what to do. After a while, he got up and went to an old woman who had been kind to him.

"Pity me," he said, "since I am very poor. I am going away now on a long journey. Make me some moccasins."

"Where are you going?" asked the old woman. "There is no war. We are very peaceful here."

"I do not know where I shall go," replied Scarface. "I am in trouble, but I cannot tell you now what it is."

This old woman had a good heart, and she liked the young man. So she made him some moccasins—seven pairs with rawhide soles. She gave him a pemmican of berries, pounded meat, and dried back fat.

All alone, and with a sad heart, he climbed the bluffs and stopped to take a last look at the camp. He wondered if he would ever see his sweetheart and his people again. "Pity me, O Sun," he prayed, and turning, he started to find the trail.

For many days, he traveled on, over great prairies, along rivers, and among the mountains. His sack of food grew lighter every day, but he saved as much of it as he could and ate berries and roots. Sometimes he killed an animal for food.

Scarface asked many animals of the forest to show him the way to the Sun's home, but none could tell him.

Told by a badger that the wolverine traveled around and had great knowledge, Scarface went to the woods and looked all around for the wolverine. He could not find him, and so he sat down to rest. He cried: "Wolverine, take pity on me. My food is gone, and my moccasins are worn out. Now I must die."

"What is it, my brother?" he heard suddenly. Looking around, he saw the animal sitting nearby.

"She whom I would marry," said Scarface, "belongs to the Sun. I am trying to find where he lives."

The wolverine answered, "I know where he lives. Wait, it is nearly night. Tomorrow I will show you the trail to the big water. He lives on the other side of it."

Early in the morning, the wolverine showed him the trail, and Scarface followed it until he came to the water's edge. Never before had he seen such a big water. The other side could not be seen. Scarface sat down on the shore. His food was all gone, and his moccasins were worn out. His heart was sick. "I cannot cross this big water," he said. "I cannot return to my people. Here, by this water, I shall die."

Two swans came swimming up to the shore. "Why have you come here?" they asked him. "What are you doing? It is very far to the place where your people live."

"I am here," replied Scarface, "to die. Far away, in my country, is a beautiful girl. I want to marry her, but she belongs to the Sun. So I started out to find him and to ask for her."

"No," said the swans, "you shall not die. Across this water is the home of that Above Person, the Sun. Get on our backs, and we will take you there."

Scarface felt strong again, and he quickly arose. He waded out into the water and lay down on the swans' backs, and they started off. Very deep and black is that fearful water. Strange people live there, and mighty animals often seize and drown a person. The swans carried him safely and took him to the other side. As they approached, Scarface saw a broad, hard trail leading away from the water's edge.

The swans told Scarface: "You are now close to the Sun's lodge. Follow that trail, and you will soon see it."

Scarface started up the trail, and pretty soon he came to some things lying in it. There was a war shirt, a shield, a bow, and arrows. He had never seen such beautiful weapons, but he did not touch them. He walked carefully around them. Farther on, he met a young man, the handsomest person he had ever seen. The young man's hair was very long, and he wore clothing made of strange skins. His moccasins were sewn with bright colored feathers. The young man asked him, "Did you see some weapons lying on the trail?"

"Yes," replied Scarface, "I saw them."

"But did you not touch them?" asked the young man.

"No, I thought someone had left them there, so I did not take them."

"You are not a thief," said the young man. "What is your name?"

"My name is Scarface."

"Where are you going?"

"I am going to the Sun."

"I am Morning Star," said the young man, "and the

Sun is my father. Come, I will take you to our lodge. My father is not at home, but he will come in at night."

Soon they came to the lodge. It was very large and handsome, and strange medicine animals were painted on it. Behind it were strange weapons and beautiful clothes—the Sun's. Scarface was ashamed to go in, but Morning Star said, "Do not be afraid, my friend, for we are glad you have come."

They entered. One person was sitting there, the Moon, who was the Sun's wife and Morning Star's mother. She spoke to Scarface kindly and gave him food. "Why have you come so far?" she asked.

Then Scarface told her about the beautiful girl he wanted to marry. "She belongs to the Sun," he said, "and I have come to ask him for her."

When it was time for the Sun to come home, the Moon hid Scarface. As soon as the Sun got to the doorway, he stopped and said, "I smell a person."

"Yes, Father," said Morning Star. "A good young man has come to see you. I know he is good, for he found some of my things on the trail and did not touch them."

Then Scarface came out from under the robes, and the Sun entered and sat down. "I am glad you have come to our lodge," he said. "Stay with us as long as you think best, for my son is lonesome sometimes."

Scarface replied, "I am here to ask you for that girl. I want to marry her. I asked her, and she was glad, but she says you own her, that you told her not to marry."

"What you say is true," said the Sun. "I have been watching her, so I know it. Now, then, I give her to you. She is yours. I am glad she has been wise. I know that she has never done wrong. The Sun blesses good women. They shall live a long time, and so shall their husbands and children. Now you will soon go home. Let me tell you something: Be wise and listen. I am the only chief. Everything is mine. I made the earth, the mountains, the prairies, the rivers, and the forests. I made the

people and all the animals. This is why I say I alone am
the chief. I can never die. True, the winter makes me old
and weak, but every summer I grow young again."

Then said the Sun: "Which one of all the animals is
smartest? The raven is, for he always finds food and is
never hungry. Which one of all the animals is most
favored by me? The buffalo is, and of all animals, I like
him best. He is for the people. He is your food and your
shelter. What part of his body is sacred? The tongue is,
and that is mine too. Come with me and see the world."
He took Scarface to the edge of the sky, and they looked
down and saw it. It is round and flat, and all around the
edge is the jumping-off place (or walls straight down.)
Then said the Sun: "When any man is sick or in danger,
his wife may promise to build me a lodge if he recovers.
If the woman is pure and true, then I will be pleased
and help the man. But if she is bad, if she lies, then I
will be angry. You shall build the lodge like the world,
round, with walls. It shall be like the sky (a hemi-
sphere), and half of it shall be painted red—that is me.
The other half you will paint black—that is the night."

Then the Sun said, "Which is the best, the heart or the
brain? The brain is, because the heart often lies, but the
brain never lies." Then he told Scarface everything about
making a Medicine Lodge. When he had finished speak-
ing, he rubbed a powerful medicine on the young man's
face, and the scar disappeared. Then he gave him two
raven feathers, saying, "These are the sign of the girl, that
I give her to you. They must always be worn by the husband of the woman who builds a Medicine Lodge."

The young man was now ready to return home.
Morning Star and the Sun gave him many beautiful
presents. The Moon cried and kissed him and called
him "my son." Then the Sun showed him the short
trail, the Wolf Road (Milky Way). He followed it and
soon reached the ground.

It was a very hot day, and all the lodge skins were

raised. The people sat in the shade. There was a chief, a very generous man, and people kept coming all day long to his lodge to feast with him. Early in the morning, this chief saw a person sitting outside nearby, tightly wrapped in his robe. The chief's friends came and went, and the sun reached the middle of the sky and passed on, down towards the mountains. Still, this person did not move. When it was almost night, the chief said, "Why does that person sit there so long? The heat has been strong, but he has not eaten nor drunk. He may be a stranger. Go and ask him in."

So, some young men went up to him and said, "Why do you sit here in the great heat? Come to the shade of the lodges. The chief asks you to feast with him."

Then the person arose and threw off his robe, and they were surprised. He wore beautiful clothes, and his bow, shield, and other weapons were of strange make. But they knew his face, although the scar was gone, and they ran ahead, shouting: "Scarface has come. He is poor no longer, and the scar on his face is gone."

All the people rushed out to see him. "Where have you been?" they asked. "Where did you get all these pretty things?" He did not answer, for he saw that there in the crowd stood the young woman. Taking the two raven feathers from his head, he gave them to her and said: "The trail was very long, and I nearly died, but with help, I found the Sun's lodge. He is glad and sends these feathers to you. They are the sign that he approves of our plan to marry."

Great was her gladness then. They were married and made the first Medicine Lodge, as the Sun had said. The Sun was glad, and he gave them great age. They were never sick, and when they were very old, one morning, their children said, "Awake, rise and eat." They did not move. In the night, in sleep, without pain, their shadows had departed for the Sand Hills.

READING FOR UNDERSTANDING

1. When her parents asked the girl why she wouldn't marry, what was her first reason? Later, what did she say was the real reason?
2. What had happened to Scarface's family? What are the Sand Hills?
3. Why do you think the girl wanted to marry Scarface? What qualities do you think she admired in him?
4. What were the conditions that the girl set for Scarface to marry her?
5. In the story, what do you think the swans may symbolize or stand for?
6. How did the Blackfoot view the Sun, the Moon, and the Morning Star? Why?
7. How did Scarface change during the course of his journey?

RESPONDING TO THE STORY

In the story, the Sun said, "Which is the best, the heart or the brain? The brain is, because the heart often lies, but the brain never lies." Some people would disagree with this statement and would trust their hearts over their minds. What do you believe, and why?

REVIEWING VOCABULARY

1. You would most likely buy *tanned* (a) gloves (b) sox (c) earrings.
2. *Relations* are people who (a) work with you (b) go to school with you (c) are part of your family.
3. A *designing* person would have a lot of (a) crayons (b) secrets (c) clothes.
4. If he *heeds* what I tell him, then he (a) pays attention (b) ignores me (c) acts confused.
5. You would find *bluffs* in the (a) ocean (b) trees (c) mountains.

6. She *waded* out into the **(a)** garage **(b)** stream **(c)** forest.

7. You would read *sacred* words in a **(a)** train schedule **(b)** prayer book **(c)** cookbook.

8. To make *pemmican*, you'll need some **(a)** motor oil **(b)** lean meat **(c)** baking soda.

THINKING CRITICALLY ABOUT CULTURE

1. What does this story tell you about the importance of the sun in the Blackfoot culture?

2. What part do you think the war shirt, the shield, and the bow and arrow played in the young man's quest?

3. Tell in your own words how this story explains the origin of the Medicine Lodge. Is this the most important aspect of the story? Why or why not?

THE DAY IT SNOWED TORTILLAS

a Spanish folktale from New Mexico

By Joe Hayes

It's almost everyone's dream to find riches. You've probably heard about the pot of gold at the end of the rainbow or the goose that laid the golden egg. Nowadays, the dream may be winning the lottery.

Some rewards require nothing more than luck—being in the right place at the right time. But holding on to your newly-found riches takes careful thought and planning. There are many ways to lose or squander your money.

In this folktale, set in New Mexico, a hard-working but simple-minded woodcutter stumbles upon a fortune. However, he could lose everything he has gained.

VOCABULARY WORDS

aghast (uh-GAST) feeling great horror or dismay
❖ She stared *aghast* at the remains of her home after the hurricane.

grumbling (GRUM-blihng) complaining
❖ He was *grumbling* that no one ever helped him do the dishes.

snore (SNAWR) breathe noisily while sleeping
❖ When she began to *snore*, I knew she had fallen asleep.

batch (BACH) quantity of items made at one time
❖ I took the *batch* of cookies out of the oven.

enthusiastically (ehn-thoo-zee-AS-tihk-lee) with eager interest
❖ When I asked if they wanted to go to the beach, the children *enthusiastically* shouted "Yes!"

embarrassed (ehm-BAR-uhst) self-conscious and uneasy
❖ I was *embarrassed* when I forgot my lines in the play.

stomped (STAHMPT) stamped with the feet
❖ He *stomped* angrily out of the room.

roughly (RUF-lee) in a harsh manner
❖ He *roughly* told the group of kids to go home.

numbskull (NUM-skul) a stupid person
❖ She felt like a *numbskull* when she failed the test.

KEY WORD

tortillas (tawr-TEE-uhs) thin, flat pancakes cooked on a griddle
❖ After she cooked the *tortillas*, she filled them with cheese.

**H**ere is a story about a poor woodcutter. He was very good at his work and could swing his ax powerfully to cut down big trees. He would split them up into firewood to sell in the village. He made a good living. But the poor man was not well-educated. He couldn't read or write and wasn't very bright. He was always doing foolish things, but he was lucky. He had a very clever wife, and she would get him out of trouble.

One day he was working far off in the mountains, and when he started home at the end of the day, he saw three leather bags by the side of the trail. He picked up the first bag and discovered that it was full of gold coins! He looked into the second, and it was full of gold too. So was the third.

He loaded the bags onto his donkey and took them home to show to his wife. She was aghast. "Don't tell anyone you found this gold!" she warned him. "It must belong to some robbers who have hidden it out in the mountains. If they find out we have it, they'll kill us to get it back!"

But then she thought, "My husband! He can never keep a secret. What shall I do?"

She came up with a plan. She told her husband, "Before you do anything else, go into the village and get me a sack of flour. I need a big sack so bring me a hundred pounds of flour."

The man went off to the village grumbling to himself, "All day I work in the mountains, and now I have to drag home a hundred pounds of flour. I'm tired of all this work." But he bought the flour and brought it home to his wife.

"Thank you," she told him. "Now, you've been working awfully hard. Why don't you go lie down?"

He liked that idea. He lay down on the bed and soon fell fast asleep. As soon as her husband began to snore, the woman went to work and began to make tortillas. She made batch after batch of tortillas until the stack reached clear up to the ceiling in the kitchen. She turned that whole hundred pounds of flour into tortillas. Then she took them outside and threw them all over the ground.

The woodcutter was so tired he slept all that evening and on through the night. He didn't wake up until morning and when he awoke, he stepped outside and saw that the ground was covered with tortillas. He called to his wife. "What's the meaning of this?" he asked.

His wife joined him at the door. "Oh, my goodness! It must have snowed tortillas last night!"

"Snowed tortillas? I've never heard of such a thing."

"What? You've never heard of it snowing tortillas? Well! You're not very well educated. You'd better go to school and learn something." So she packed him a lunch, dressed him up, and sent him off to school.

He didn't know how to read or write, so they put him in the first grade where he had to squeeze into one of the little chairs the children sat in. The teacher asked questions and the children raised their hands enthusiastically. Because he didn't know the answers to any of those questions, he grew more and more embarrassed. Then he had to go to the blackboard and write, even though he didn't know the alphabet. The little boy beside him began to write his name on the board, and the woodcutter tried to copy the boy's letters. When the other children saw the man writing the boy's name instead of his own, they began to laugh at him.

He couldn't stand it any longer so he stomped out of the school and hurried home. He seized his ax. "I've had enough of education," he told his wife. "I'm going to go cut firewood."

"Fine," she called after him. "You go do your work."

About a week later, just as the woman had suspected, the robbers showed up at the house. "Where is that gold your husband found?" they demanded.

The wife acted innocent. "Gold?" She shook her head. "I don't know anything about any gold."

"Come on!" the robbers said. "Your husband's been telling everyone in the village he found three sacks of gold, and those sacks belong to us. You'd better give them back."

She looked disgusted. "Did my husband say that? Oh, that man! He says the strangest things! I don't know anything about your gold."

"That's a likely story. We'll find out by waiting here until he comes home." So the robbers waited around all day—sharpening their knives and cleaning their pistols.

Toward evening the woodcutter came up the trail with his donkey. The robbers ran out and grabbed him roughly. "Where's that gold you found?"

The woodcutter scratched his head. "Gold?" he mumbled. "Oh, yes, now I remember. My wife hid it." He called out, "Wife, what did you do with that gold?"

His wife sounded puzzled. "What gold? I don't know what you're talking about."

"Sure you do. Remember? It was the day before it snowed tortillas and I came home with three bags of gold. Then in the morning you sent me to school."

The robbers looked at one another. "Did he say, 'snowed tortillas'?" they whispered. "She sent him to school? They shook their heads in dismay. "Why did we waste our time with this numbskull? He's out of his head." And they went away thinking the woodcutter was crazy and had just been talking a lot of nonsense.

From that day on, it didn't really matter whether he was well-educated or clever. It didn't even matter if he was a good woodcutter, for he was a rich man. He and his wife had those three sacks of gold all to themselves, and the robbers never came back.

READING FOR UNDERSTANDING

1. What was the reaction of the woodcutter's wife when her husband brought the gold home? What did she decide to do?

2. Why did the wife decide it was important for her husband to lie down and rest? What happened when he awoke?

3. The wife said he should go to school, but when the woodcutter came home and said he'd had enough, she wasn't angry. Why not?

4. In what way did the robbers help the woodcutter's wife carry out her plan?

5. Did it really snow tortillas as in the story? Why did the wife make it look as though it had?

6. Do you think the woodcutter and his wife lived happily ever after? Why or why not?

RESPONDING TO THE STORY

In this story, the woodcutter's wife didn't tell him her plan for keeping the gold. Why do you think she kept it from him? Do you think there are times when people shouldn't be honest with one another? Explain.

REVIEWING VOCABULARY

Match each word on the left with the correct definition on the right.

1. aghast
2. grumbling
3. snore
4. batch
5. enthusiastically
6. embarassed
7. stomped
8. roughly
9. numbskull
10. tortillas

a. self-conscious or uneasy
b. quantity of items made at one time
c. stamped with the feet
d. thin, flat pancakes cooked on a griddle
e. complaining
f. feeling horror or dismay
g. in a harsh manner
h. breathe noisily while sleeping
i. with eager interest
j. stupid person

THINKING CRITICALLY

1. How does this folktale support the belief that those who are good will be rewarded and those who are bad will be punished? Explain, using story details.

2. List the qualities of the woodcutter and his wife. Compare and contrast them to show how a successful relationship depends on a balance of personalities.

3. Often, people who are limited in some ways are successful in other ways. Describe a good example of this, based on a character you have read about or seen in a film.

THE CRADLE DIDN'T ROCK

an African American tale

Retold by Julius Lester

Brer Rabbit is one of the popular animal characters in the collection of folktales written down and published in the late 1800s by Joel Chandler Harris. The Brer Rabbit stories are an important part of the literary and historical tradition of the southeastern United States. Brought from Africa, the animal characters in these stories personified human traits. Brer Rabbit as the trickster was held in high esteem because of his cunning and deception—skills the slaves often found necessary for survival in the Americas.

"The Cradle Didn't Rock" and many other Brer Rabbit tales were retold by Julius Lester. In this version, he has kept some of the language of the original retellings.

VOCABULARY WORDS

racket (RAK-iht) loud noise
❖ Busy carpenters made quite a *racket*.

trigger (TRIHG-uhr) small lever that releases a spring when pressed
❖ The fox stepped on the *trigger*, and the trap snapped shut on its leg.

plumb (PLUM) [dialect] entirely; absolutely
❖ Shopping all day long has left me *plumb* tired!

twitching (TWIHCH-ihng) moving with quick, slight jerks
❖ The angry cat's tail was *twitching*.

varmints (VAHR-muhnts) [dialect] objectionable animals, such as rats
❖ The farmer aimed his gun at the crows and shouted, "I'll get you *varmints* if it's the last thing I do!"

yonder (YAHN-duhr) there, but at a distance
❖ There is a pond over *yonder* in the woods.

young'uns (YUNG-uhnz) [dialect: "young ones"] children
❖ She said she would feed the *young'uns* first.

slats (SLATS) thin, narrow strips of wood or metal.
❖ The children peeked through the *slats* of the fence.

squinch (SKWIHNCH) [dialect] squint; to look with the eyes partly closed
❖ I saw him *squinch* his eyes when he had trouble reading the sign.

**M**r. Man got sick and tired of Brer Rabbit and his tricks, so he built a trap to take care of him once and for all. Back in them days folks didn't know too much about carpentering, since it had just been invented. They did the best they could, which wasn't none too good if you want to know the truth. So Mr. Man's trap was near about as big as a shed and way too big for Brer Rabbit.

He was making so much racket and doing so much cussing while he was building the trap that it attracted Brer Rabbit's attention. Brer Rabbit couldn't make no sense at all out of what Mr. Man was building, but he kept an eye on him. Don't nobody be building nothing just 'cause it's a sunny day.

When Mr. Man finished, he carried it out in the woods. Brer Rabbit watched Mr. Man put some bait in it and set the trigger. Mr. Man stepped back and smiled admiringly at his trap. Brer Rabbit smiled too.

Now he had a problem. How was he going to get something in the trap so Mr. Man wouldn't be disappointed?

Brer Rabbit set off down the road. Before long he ran into Brer Wolf. They passed the time of day and when Brer Rabbit said he was troubled in his mind, Brer Wolf asked him how come.

"Nothing is going right these days. I just feel plumb wore out."

Brer Wolf's eyes gleamed and his taste buds set to quivering. But he pretended to be sympathetic. "I ain't never heard you talk this way, Brer Rabbit. Why don't you tell me about it? Maybe it make you feel better to talk about it. If there's anything I can do to help you out, I be glad to do it. I'll put my heart into it too." Brer Wolf grinned and his nose started twitching.

Brer Rabbit make like he don't notice. "Well, I'll tell

you about it and see what you think. Mr. Man hired me to sit up nights and keep all the creatures and varmints out of his vegetable garden. He say I done such a good job that, in addition to all the greens I can eat from his garden every day, he'd like to make me a cradle for my little ones. He give it to me this morning, but it's so big and heavy, I had to leave it back yonder there in the woods. I just don't know how I'm ever going to get it home."

Brer Wolf was a little jealous. His ole woman had been on him about getting a cradle for their young'uns. "My wife say cradles is the latest fashion."

"They is, but to tell the truth, I don't care nothing about no cradle. I was only taking this one because Mr. Man was nice enough to make it for me."

"Well, if you don't want it, Brer Rabbit, I be glad to take it off your hands."

Brer Rabbit thought about it for a minute. "Well, the cradle is too big for my young'uns anyway, and just about the right size for yours."

Brer Rabbit took Brer Wolf to where Mr. Man had set the trap.

"There's your cradle, Brer Wolf."

Brer Wolf walked around it. "What's that on the inside?"

"Them's the rockers. It's the latest fashion."

Brer Wolf walked in the trap, sprung the trigger, and there he was.

Brer Rabbit laughed and ducked into the weeds, and not a minute too soon because Mr. Man came up the path to check on his trap. He looked through the slats and clapped his hands. "I got you now! I got you and you ain't getting away this time."

"Got who?" came Brer Wolf's muffled voice from inside. "Who you think you got?"

"I don't think, 'cause I know! Brer Rabbit! That's who!"

"Let me out of here and I'll show you who I am."

Mr. Man laughed and laughed. "You can't change your voice and fool me, Brer Rabbit."

"I ain't Brer Rabbit."

Mr. Man looked through the crack again and saw some short ears. "You may have cut off your ears, but I'd know you anywhere. And I see that you sharpened your teeth, but you can't fool me."

"Ain't nobody trying to fool you, fool! I ain't Brer Rabbit! Look at my nice, bushy tail."

"Uh-huh. You went and tied a tail onto your behind, but you can't fool me, Brer Rabbit."

"I ain't trying to fool you. Look at the hair on my back. That don't look like Brer Rabbit, do it?"

"So you went and rolled in some red sand. You still Brer Rabbit!"

"Look at my black legs. Do they look like Brer Rabbit?"

"Naw, but you put smut on your legs to try and fool me."

Brer Wolf was desperate now. "Look at my green eyes. Do they look like Brer Rabbit's?"

"You can squinch your eyes and make 'em look any way you want, Brer Rabbit. But you can't fool me."

"I AIN'T BRER RABBIT! I AIN'T BRER RABBIT! AND YOU BETTER LET ME OUT OF HERE SO I CAN SKIN THE HIDE OFF BRER RABBIT MY OWN-SELF!"

Mr. Man just laughed and laughed and po' Brer Wolf sat down and cried like a baby.

READING FOR UNDERSTANDING

1. Why did Mr. Man build a trap? How did Brer Rabbit find out about it?
2. After Mr. Man set the trap, Brer Rabbit smiled. Why did he smile, and what did he decide to do? What does that tell you about his relationship with Mr. Man?
3. When Brer Rabbit told Brer Wolf how tired he was, how did Brer Wolf react? Why did he pretend to be sympathetic?
4. Describe how Brer Rabbit tricked Brer Wolf. Do you think Brer Rabbit is often successful in getting what he needs? Explain.
5. Why do you think the man in the tale was called "Mr. Man"? What does this tell you about his relationship to Brer Rabbit and Brer Wolf?

RESPONDING TO THE STORY

Mr. Man was so sure that he had trapped Brer Rabbit that no matter how much evidence Brer Wolf gave him, he didn't want to believe him. Have you ever been in a situation where you wanted something so much that nothing anyone said against it could make you change your mind? Describe what happened and how you felt.

REVIEWING VOCABULARY

1. He made a *racket* by **(a)** knitting **(b)** cooking **(c)** hammering.
2. A *trigger* is found in a **(a)** trap **(b)** book **(c)** hammer.
3. If I feel *plumb* tired, I am **(a)** not tired **(b)** a little tired **(c)** very tired.
4. A *twitching* foot is **(a)** itching **(b)** sweating **(c)** moving.
5. **(a)** Rats **(b)** Dogs **(c)** Cows are *varmints*.

6. If my cabin is *yonder*, it's **(a)** right here **(b)** over there **(c)** not there.

7. When his mother referred to the *"young'uns"*, she was talking about **(a)** her children **(b)** her parents **(c)** her pets.

8. *Slats* are **(a)** fuzzy balls of yarn **(b)** thin strips of wood **(c)** short pieces of straw.

9. If you *squinch* your eyes, they are **(a)** wide open **(b)** partly closed **(c)** shut tight.

THINKING CRITICALLY

1. In what way is the end of this story similar to and different from "Little Red Riding Hood"?

2. Brer Rabbit gets the better of Brer Wolf by tricking him into thinking that the trap is a cradle. Many other stories in this book have trickster characters. You may wish to read some of them, beginning on pages 93, 121, and 180. As you read, identify the trickster character and the trick played. Decide which trick is most successful and explain why.

3. What human personality traits are represented by Brer Rabbit and Brer Wolf? Do you think the author has used personification effectively in this story? Explain.

OJEEG, THE HUNTER, AND THE ICE MAN
from the Micmac of Canada
Retold by Dorothy de Wit

The following tale is told by the Micmac, a Native American people in eastern Canada in the region around Quebec and New Brunswick. Long ago, like the Eskimo, the Micmac depended on animals for food, clothing, and shelter. In winter they hunted caribou, moose, and small game. In summer they fished, gathered shellfish, and hunted seals on the coast.

The Micmac people lived a difficult life in an area where the winters are very harsh. Heavy snowfall and months of subfreezing temperatures gave the Micmac a healthy respect for and fear of winter.

Sometimes the snowstorms and bitter winds forced them to take shelter for days. You can imagine how important fire was to these people, as well as the necessity of stocking up on food and fuel. The Micmac believed in a world where everything in nature has a spirit. They saw their challenging environment in these spiritual terms. Read on to see how each winter became a test of survival against a powerful spirit, the "Ice Man."

VOCABULARY WORDS

bitter (BIHT-uhr) severe; harsh
❖ Last winter was *bitter* in the Northeast.

vanquish (VAN-kwihsh) defeat in battle
❖ The king sent his soldiers to *vanquish* the enemy.

pummeled (PUM-uhld) hit over and over again
❖ The bully *pummeled* the boy until he ran away.

jostled (JAHS-uhld) pushed, shoved, bumped into
❖ She *jostled* a few people, as she made her way to the front of the room.

resin (REHZ-uhn) sticky substance found in trees and plants
❖ When they cut into the tree, *resin* began to ooze out.

extracted (ehk-STRAK-tehd) removed
❖ The bad tooth had to be *extracted* at once.

rendered (REHN-duhrd) melted down
❖ He *rendered* the fat and stored it in jars.

flaunted (FLAWN-tuhd) made a showy display
❖ She *flaunted* her engagement ring in front of her friends.

hardy (HAHR-dee) strong; able to survive
❖ The *hardy* birds do not fly south for the winter.

**On the shores** of a large body of water, near the great evergreen forests of the north, there lived a hunter with his wife and young son. Their wigwam stood by itself, far from the village, and they were very content, for Ojeeg was skilled with his arrows and brought as much game and furs to his wife as they had need of! The little boy would have been happy, indeed, if the snow had not been so deep or the winters so long. He did not miss companions to play with, for his father showed him the tracks of the grouse and the squirrels. He pointed out the white coats of the rabbits and the weasel, and he trained him to use his bow carefully so that he would not waste his arrows.

But the cold grew more bitter as the long winter months dragged on. One day the boy saw a squirrel running around a stump, looking vainly for buried nuts, for the snow was too deep. Finally, the squirrel rested on his bushy tail, and as the boy came toward him, he said, "I am hungry, and there is no food to be found anywhere! Aren't you, too, tired of this ice and cold?"

"I am," said the hunter's son. "But what can we do against the power of the Ice Man? We are weak; he is cruel and strong!"

"You can cry! You can howl with hunger!" replied the squirrel. "Your father is a great hunter. He has strong power, and maybe he can vanquish the Ice Man if he sees your grief. Cry, cry, small brother! It may help!"

That night the young boy came into the wigwam, threw down his bow and arrows, and huddled beside the fire, sobbing. He would not answer his mother when she questioned him, and he would not stop crying. When his father came home, the boy's cries grew even louder, and nothing would make him stop, until at last the hunter asked, "Is it perhaps that you are lonely? That you do not like the snow and the cold?" At that the boy nodded his head. "Then," said the father, "I shall see if I have the power to change it."

He went out the next day on his snowshoes. Long he traveled by the frozen water till he came to a narrow place that was choked with huge blocks of ice. He took his sharp knife and a stone chisel, and he began to dig away at chunks. Many hours he chopped and hacked and pummeled the ice, and in the end he heard the barricade crack! The ice began to move, and a part of it broke off and jostled and bumped around until more cracks appeared. The whole mass of ice began to float slowly away. The hunter rested and wiped the sweat from his face. Then he heard the voice of Peboan, the ice king, piercing the air: "You have won for now, my son! You are strong indeed, and your Manito power is great! But I shall gain the final victory, for next year I will return, and I will bring even more snow! The North Wind will blow more fiercely, and the trees will break with the weight of the ice I will pile on their branches! The waters will freeze so that no matter how many warriors cross them, not a crack will appear. Then you will see, grandson, who is the master of winter!"

The hunter returned to his wigwam. The snows were melting, and green was returning to the earth. Sweet sap rose in the maple trees, and his little son shouted with joy! But the hunter remembered the threat which the ice king had made: "Next winter will be worse—much worse!"

So he set himself to cutting wood and piling it in great stacks; he gathered the resin from the pine trees and formed it into great lumps. From the game which he brought home he extracted much fat, and this he rendered and stored in large oil pots. Baskets of evergreen cones and thick logs he stored up also. Then, when the maple and the oak flaunted their red and yellow banners at the dark hemlocks, he went somewhat apart from his own lodging and built a small, very tight new wigwam.

He left his wife warm skins and food in quantity; then, with supplies for himself, he began stacking them, and the firewood, the resin lumps, the oil pots, and the baskets of cones, within his new lodging.

When the first snowfall whitened the ground, he bade his wife and son have courage and went to the new wigwam. He laced the skins tightly and closed the opening securely. With food and water at hand and warm furs to cover him, he built a very small fire in the center of the fire hold and sat down to wait for Peboan.

At first the frost was light, and the snow melted quickly. At night the wind did not rise much, and the hunter thought, "Perhaps I have frightened old Peboan away! He will see that it is not so easy to win over me!" But as the winter deepened, the tent poles rattled more, the skins shuddered a bit, and it took more fire to warm the wigwam. Still, Peboan did not come. The hunter heard the great owl swoop through the trees at night. He heard weasels and rabbits move through the snow, and once the heavy footfall of a moose crashed through the drifts. The cold became intense.

Then, suddenly one night, the skins across the door opening were torn away and a gust of North Wind almost blew the fire apart! Peboan stood there, grizzled and bent. His face was lined and cruel, and his long beard hung with icicles. "I have come as I said I would," he shouted.

The hunter rose swiftly, tied up the door skins, and put more wood on the fire. A chill ran through him— the ice king's power was very great! "Grandfather, be seated at my fire. You are my guest here!" he said. The old one sat far from the fire and watched him.

"My power is great! I blow my breath—the streams stand still; the waters are stiff and hard like rock crystal!"

The hunter shivered and put another log on the fire. "The snow covers the land when I shake my head; trees are without any leaves, and their branches break with the weight of my ice!"

The hunter added some cones, and the flames leaped up. "No birds fly now, for they have gone far away. Only the hardy ones flit around, and they are hungry."

The hunter added more wood to the fire, for the air in the wigwam was becoming bitter cold, and frost hung on his eyebrows and nose. "The animals hide away and sleep through the long cold." Peboan laughed grimly as he saw the man draw his fur closer around him.

"Even the hunters do not leave their lodges. The children curl deep into their blankets for warmth and cry with hunger."

Then Ojeeg pulled out the resin lumps; first one, then another he tossed into the coals, and they burned hotly. Peboan shook his white head and moved as far away from the heat as he could. When the hunter saw that, he added yet another clutch of pitch and more logs. Sweat began to roll down the wrinkled face; the ice king huddled close to the wall of the wigwam; his icy garments began to melt.

Ojeeg took up the pots of oil and poured them into the fire. The flames burned orange and red and blue! They licked at the old man's long robe, at his ice-covered feet, at his snowy mantle, and the Ice Man cried out in pain, "Enough, enough! I have seen your power, Ojeeg! Take back your fire and heat! Stifle your flames!" But the hunter only built up the fire higher, and the Ice Man became smaller and smaller, till at last he melted into a pool of water which ran over the ground and out, under the wigwam opening. When he saw that, Ojeeg, the hunter, untied the skins and looked out. The Ice Man was gone completely! Beyond his doorway the ground was brown and soft with pine needles, he could hear running water, and birds flew through the treetops. How long had he been in his wigwam? The spring was at hand!

Ojeeg put out his fire and ran toward his wife and son, who had come out and stood waiting to welcome him! The ice king would not make so long a visit next year! Only the white flowers of the snowdrop, fragile and small, remained to mark where Peboan had left his footprints!

READING FOR UNDERSTANDING

The following paragraph summarizes the story. Decide which of the words below best fits in each blank. Some words are not used, and some words are used more than once. Write your answers on a separate sheet of paper.

A hunter named **(1)**_____ lived with his family in a **(2)**_____ far from the village. As the winter grew colder, his **(3)**_____ became more unhappy. A **(4)**_____ told the hunter's **(5)**_____ to cry so that **(6)**_____ would battle the power of the **(7)**_____. When **(8)**_____ broke up the ice, the **(9)**_____ grew angry and said that the next winter would be worse. So Ojeeg went home and began to prepare for the coming winter by cutting **(10)**_____ and gathering resin and fat. He then built a **(11)**_____ and stocked it with all the supplies. At the first snow, he went there to wait for the **(12)**_____. When he finally appeared, in a great gust of **(13)**_____, the hunter asked him to sit at the **(14)**_____. The hunter then made it hotter and hotter until the **(15)**_____ cried out and melted. When **(16)**_____ left the wigwam and saw his family, it was **(17)**_____.

Words: *fire, Ice Man, North Wind, Ojeeg, rabbit, son, spring, squirrel, summer, wife, wigwam, wood*

RESPONDING TO THE STORY

This story provides a brief but vivid picture of the lives of the Micmac people. Select a scene that you thought stood out from the rest, and write a paragraph telling why you liked it. What details stood out and made it memorable for you?

REVIEWING VOCABULARY

1. A *bitter* wind is **(a)** mild **(b)** severe **(c)** loud.
2. If you *vanquish* the enemy, then you **(a)** meet it **(b)** run away from it **(c)** defeat it.
3. When he *pummeled* the pillow, he **(a)** sat on it **(b)** hit it many times **(c)** put it on the sofa.
4. If I *jostled* some people, I **(a)** bumped into them **(b)** yelled at them **(c)** laughed at them.
5. *Resin* is found in **(a)** rocks **(b)** trees **(c)** animals.
6. If a tooth is *extracted*, it is **(a)** pulled **(b)** lost **(c)** fixed.
7. When she *rendered* the fat, it **(a)** melted **(b)** hardened **(c)** disappeared.
8. If I *flaunted* my new car, I **(a)** had an accident in it **(b)** showed it off to my friends **(c)** had it checked over.
9. You would expect something that is *hardy* to **(a)** die from a disease **(b)** live for a short time **(c)** last for a long time.

THINKING CRITICALLY ABOUT CULTURE

1. The squirrel called the little boy "small brother," and Ojeeg called the Ice Man "grandfather." What does this tell you about the way the Micmac viewed their relationships with animals and the spirit world?
2. Discuss the relationships between Ojeeg and his family. Why do you think he built the special lodging and stayed in it alone to meet the Ice Man?
3. We can't control nature. We can only learn from it and adapt to it. Explain how the myth supports this statement.

THE MAIZE SPIRIT

a Chippewa tale

Retold by Lewis Spence

The Chippewa, Native Americans who are also known as the Ojibwa, have always lived in the Great Lakes area. Now they live as far west as Montana. In the past, they mainly lived on deer, fish, corn, squash, and wild rice. Corn, also called maize, was the most important food for the Native Americans because it could be easily cultivated as a crop. Corn could be eaten fresh and, more importantly, its seeds could be ground into meal. The ground meal could be dried and stored and eaten at a later time. This story tells about how maize was given to the Chippewa.

In the story, you will read about a teenage boy who undergoes a special ritual. Like other boys his age, he must go into the woods alone and fast for several days. The ritual was an initiation into manhood. The Chippewa believed that spending time alone without food was supposed to cause reflection and bring on dreams that increased wisdom and strength of spirit. In this story, these visions turn out to be very important indeed.

You may wish to compare this story with "Why Corn Has White Silky Hair." After you have read both stories, think about how each retelling reflects its culture of origin.

VOCABULARY WORDS

disposition (dihs-puh-ZIHSH-uhn) one's natural way of acting toward others
❖ Everyone agreed that he had the nicest *disposition*.

fast (FAST) the act of going without food for a period of time
❖ She knew that a *fast* was not a healthy way to lose weight.

remote (rih-MOHT) far off and hidden away
❖ They found a *remote* cabin in the woods.

ordeal (awr-DEEL) a difficult or painful experience
❖ Working long hours in a hospital emergency room can be an *ordeal*.

meditating (MEHD-uh-tay-tihng) thinking quietly; reflecting
❖ She found that *meditating* for a short time helped her to relax in times of stress.

revealed (rih-VEELD) made known
❖ When he *revealed* my secret, he was no longer my friend.

summoned (SUM-uhnd) sent for; ordered to appear
❖ The bell *summoned* us to the dinner table.

slay (SLAY) kill in a violent way
❖ The king sent his men to *slay* the dragon.

A boy of fourteen or fifteen dwelt with his parents, brothers, and sisters in a lodge deep in the woods. The family, though poor, were very happy and contented. The father was a hunter of courage and skill. There were times, however, when he could barely supply the needs of his family. Since none of his children was old enough to help, times were hard.

The boy was of a cheerful disposition, like his father, and his great desire was to benefit his people. The time had come for him to observe the initial fast required of all Indian boys of his age. His mother made him a little fasting lodge in a remote spot where he would not be interrupted during his ordeal.

The boy stayed there, meditating on the goodness of the Great Spirit, who had made all things beautiful for the enjoyment of people. The boy prayed that some way to help his people might be revealed to him in a dream.

On the third day of his fast he was too weak to ramble through the forest. As he lay in a state between sleeping and waking, a beautiful youth, richly dressed in green robes, and wearing on his head wonderful green plumes, came toward him.

"The Great Spirit has heard your prayers," said the youth. His voice was like the sound of the wind sighing through the grass. "Listen to me and you shall have your desire fulfilled. Arise and wrestle with me."

The boy obeyed. Though his limbs were weak, his brain was clear and active. He felt he could not but obey the soft-voiced stranger. After a long, silent struggle, the stranger said:

"That will do for today. Tomorrow I shall come again."

The boy lay back exhausted, but on the next day the green-clad stranger reappeared. The conflict was renewed. As the struggle went on, the youth felt himself grow stronger and more confident. Before leaving

him for the second time, the visitor offered him some
words of praise and encouragement.

On the third day the youth, pale and feeble, was
again summoned to the contest. As he grasped his
opponent, the very contact seemed to give him new
strength. He fought more and more bravely, till his
companion cried out that he had had enough. Before
he took his departure, the visitor told the boy the following day would be the last contest.

"Tomorrow," said he, "your father will bring you
food, and that will help you. In the evening I shall
come and wrestle with you. I know that you are des-
tined to succeed and to obtain your heart's desire.
When you have thrown me, strip off my garments and
plumes. Bury me where I fall and keep the earth above
me moist and clean. Once a month, let my remains be
covered with fresh earth. You shall see me again, and I
will be clothed in my green garments and plumes." So

saying, he vanished.

Next day the boy's father brought him food. The youth, however, begged to set it aside till evening. Once again the stranger appeared. Though he had eaten nothing, the hero's strength, as before, seemed to increase as he struggled. At length he threw his opponent. Then he stripped off his garments and plumes and buried him in the earth. He was sorry to slay such a beautiful youth.

His task done, he returned to his parents. He soon recovered his full strength. He never forgot the grave of his friend, however. Not a weed was allowed to grow on it. Finally he was rewarded by seeing the green plumes rise above the earth and broaden out into graceful leaves. When the fall came, he requested his father to see the grave. By this time the plant was at its full height, tall and beautiful, with waving leaves and golden tassels. The father was filled with surprise and admiration.

"It is my friend," murmured the youth, "the friend of my dreams."

"It is *Mon-da-min*," said his father, "the spirit's grain, the gift of the Great Spirit."

And in this manner maize was given to the Indians.

READING FOR UNDERSTANDING

1. Describe the life of this Chippewa teenager. Refer to details in the story.

2. What was the boy's great desire? Why?

3. Who appeared to him during his fast? What did he want the boy to do?

4. The myth says that the youth's voice was "like the sound of the wind sighing through the grass." How did the boy's voice sound? Why do you think he sounded this way?

5. When the father brought his son food, why do you think the boy set it aside till evening?

6. Explain how the boy achieved his desire, and why it was important.

RESPONDING TO THE STORY

For this Chippewa teenager, fasting alone in the woods was an initiation rite for becoming a man. What are some "rites of passage" for teenagers in our culture? Are there any special ceremonies or traditions?

REVIEWING VOCABULARY

The following sentences are based on the story. Decide which of the words following the sentences best fits each blank. Some of the words are not used. Write your answers on a separate sheet of paper.

1. The boy in this myth had a very cheerful _____.

2. Like all Chippewa boys his age, he went on a _____.

3. The difficult _____ took place in a _____ area.

4. While he was _____ on the Great Spirit, he prayed that a way to help his people would be _____ to him in a dream.

5. A youth dressed in green _____ him to a contest.

6. He was very sorry to _____ this youth.

Words: *disposition, fast, meditating, ordeal, prayer, remote, revealed, sighing, skill, slay, summoned*

THINKING CRITICALLY ABOUT CULTURE

1. Each Native American nation has stories that reflect what is important to that people. What did you learn about the Chippewa from this story? What did they consider important?

2. Describe the boy's fasting ritual. Why did he do it? What did he hope would happen? How was this experience a reflection of the Chippewa culture? What part did the vision play in preparing the boy for adulthood?

4. The growing of corn was was important in many cultures in the Americas. After reading the next story in this book, "Why Corn Has Silky White Hair," compare how each storyteller has approached the topic. Do you prefer one retelling to the other? Why?

WHY CORN HAS SILKY WHITE HAIR
a Southern United States tale
Retold by Anne Pellowski

Dialect reflects the natural way people talk to each other in a particular region. People in different parts of a country might pronounce the same words differently. They might also phrase their sentences differently and even use some different words. The person who writes the story down tries to reproduce dialect in print.

Within the United States, there are several regions, each with its own dialects, including Northern, Midwestern, and Southern. As you read this myth from the South, see how the use of dialect affects the story. You might want to try reading it aloud for full effect.

VOCABULARY WORDS

tend (TEHND) take care of; look after
❖ One of the boy's chores was to *tend* the chickens.

dew (DOO) moisture in small drops
❖ The sunlight made the *dew* on the grass sparkle.

schedule (SKEH-jool) list
❖ The waitress checked the *schedule* to see which days she had to work.

impression (ihm-PREHSH-uhn) effect produced on a person
❖ He gave us the *impression* that he wanted to join us.

rheumatism (ROO-muh-tihz-uhm) painful condition of the joints and muscles
❖ Because of her *rheumatism,* she found it hard to go up and down the stairs.

dim (DIHM) not clear; weak
❖ I needed glasses because my eyesight was getting *dim.*

sowed (SOHD) planted seeds
❖ The farmer *sowed* the corn in early spring.

scragglier (SKRAG-lee-uhr) more uneven in growth
❖ His beard was quite scraggly, but his brother's beard was even *scragglier.*

**O**nce there was an old man who never did see fit to think that one day he was goin' to die.

One day Old Man was on the porch in his rockin' chair and he see someone walkin' up the path to the house. "Evenin'," he called out, "you a stranger 'round here?"

"Evenin' Old Man," the stranger say. "No, I ain't no real stranger 'round here. Come through this way every once in a while. My name is Death."

When Old Man hear that, he stop rockin'. "Well, evenin', Death. Didn't expect you. You got business 'round here?"

"Funny how lots of folks don't expect me," Death say. "Yes, I am on business, Old Man. I come for you. Put on your hat and let's go."

Old Man he didn't want to go. He liked it fine where he was. He say, "Yes, sir, Death, thank you kindly. Mighty fine of you comin' all this way. But I sure could use a little more time. I got a big field of corn out there to take care of. Maybe you could stop by again in two—three weeks?"

"Well," Death say, "go tend your corn, and I'll be back next Saturday." Death went off elsewhere.

Three—four days went by, and on Saturday mornin' the old man was in the cornfield pullin' weeds. He heard the cornstalks rustlin', and Death was standin' there. "Well, come on, Old Man," Death say, "I'm real busy this mornin' and I can't stand around."

"Good mornin', Death," Old Man say. "It's a fine mornin'. This dew on the ground makes it good for pullin' weeds. How'd you like to give me a hand?"

Death got kind of mad when he hear that. "Now look here, Old Man, I ain't no field hand. I got my own work to do. I got a regular schedule to fill."

"Death," Old Man say, "I wonder can you give me a

little more time? Folks has a big need for corn, you know, and this field needs lots of attention."

"All right, then," Death say, "get on with your weed-in'. I'll pick you up next turn around."

"You do that," Old Man say, "just drop in next time you're in the neighborhood." When Death went away, the old man went back to weedin' the corn field. Fact that Death kept comin' back didn't make no impression on him. He didn't do nothin' to get ready, just went ahead like he always did. Winter went past and the old man forgot all about Death. But he was beginnin' to feel mighty poorly. His rheumatism was gettin' worse. His eyes was gettin' more dim, and he didn't hear so good.

Next spring Death came along. "Come on, Old Man," he say, "it's time."

"Mornin', Death," Old Man say. "Have a chair and rest yourself."

"Now, look here, Old Man," Death say, "I'm real busy and you foolin' me. Put on your hat and come on."

Old Man didn't want to go along this time any more'n last time. "Tell you what," he say. "I'm mighty sorry to see you makin' all these trips, and I'm goin' to make it easy for you. You just get on with your work, and next time you figure you need me you can send me a sign and I'll come. Save you a lot of walkin'."

"What kind of sign?" Death ask him.

"A sign I can see or a sign I can hear," Old Man say, "either one. That'll give me time to get this corn crop sowed."

"That's a promise, ain't it?" Death say.

"It's a promise," Old Man tell him, "in the name of the Good Book."

"All right then," Death say. "When you hear the sign or see the sign, just put on your hat and come on."

"So long," Old Man say.

Old Man was mighty old by then. He got to feelin'

more and more poorly. His eyes got dimmer and his ears got weaker, and in two—three months he couldn't neither see nor hear a thing. He was deaf and blind.

One mornin' a letter come. It was a sign from Death. But the Old Man couldn't read it, 'cause he was blind. Four—five days later Death sent a messenger to tell the old man: "Death sent me to give you the sign to hear." But the old man couldn't hear a word, so he didn't put on his hat and go.

So Death came himself. He looked and saw the old man was deaf and blind and couldn't neither see a sign nor hear it. He was mad. "You fooled me, Old Man," he say. "I'm not comin' back no more."

The old man got more poorly all the time, but he didn't die, 'cause Death had passed him by. His beard got longer and scragglier all the time, and he wasted away till there wasn't hardly nothin' to him. He kept tendin' his corn, but he couldn't see where he was goin' and got to fallin' and tanglin' up with the stalks. He got so thin and poorly one day he just disappeared altogether.

But if you look on the corn ears you can see that there's some white hair hangin' on the ends. That's some of the Old Man's whiskers he lost whilst fallin' around 'mongst the cornstalks.

Folks say he never did die, just disappeared.

READING FOR UNDERSTANDING

1. Describe briefly the first meeting of Death and the Old Man. How did the Old Man react?

2. What do you think Death meant when he said that he "ain't no real stranger 'round here"?

3. Why do you think Death was willing to come back? How did Death's reaction change over time?

4. The Old Man realized that he could delay Death only for a short time. What were some of the signs he had of approaching death?

5. Does this myth, or tale, have a main theme? What is it?

6. Other stories in this book describe the origins of things in nature. Read some of them on pages 40, 62, and 195 and identify what each story explains.

RESPONDING TO THE MYTH

There is a saying that goes: "You can catch more flies with honey than with vinegar." How did Old Man show he believed in that? In what other ways might he have dealt with his situation?

REVIEWING VOCABULARY

1. You would have to *tend* **(a)** a movie **(b)** a meal **(c)** a pet.

2. *Dew* is found in **(a)** wet grass in the morning **(b)** a dry desert in the afternoon **(c)** a covering of snow at night.

3. A *schedule* is a **(a)** plan **(b)** cookbook **(c)** thermometer.

4. He gave the *impression* he was sad by **(a)** saying he was sad **(b)** saying he wasn't sad **(c)** looking like he was sad.
5. A person with *rheumatism* would usually **(a)** run a race **(b)** have physical pain **(c)** predict the future.
6. Because her eyesight was *dim,* she **(a)** drove a bus **(b)** used a lamp **(c)** painted pictures.
7. A farmer who *sowed* corn **(a)** planted it **(b)** ground it **(c)** picked it.
8. If my neighbor's lawn is *scragglier* than mine, the neighbor's grass looks **(a)** much greener **(b)** better watered **(c)** more uneven.

THINKING CRITICALLY

1. Did the dialect get easier to understand as you got further into the story? What happened when you read the story aloud? Why do you think the story-teller might have decided to use dialect to tell this story?
2. The way the old man talks to Death is very revealing of his character. What is the man like? Support this statement with evidence from the story.
3. The story ends with "Folks say he never did die, just disappeared." Suggest why the story ends in this way. How do you think someone came up with the idea for this myth?

GINGER FOR THE HEART

a story of Chinese immigrants in the New World

By Paul Yee

This folktale takes place in a Chinatown in California, during the time of the Gold Rush in the middle 1800s. When gold was discovered, many people in the nation moved west in the hopes of striking it rich.

Folktales of Chinese Americans strongly reflect the traditions and beliefs of the Chinese, both ancient and modern. In this story, we see the traditional Chinese dedication of a woman to her family. We also see her promise to wait for the return of the man she loves.

Yenna, the beautiful woman with a good heart, says good-bye to her true love when he joins the others in a search for gold. She also gives him an unusual farewell gift—a ginger root—and says that she will await his return.

VOCABULARY WORDS

ebony (EHB-uh-nee) a hard, black wood
❖ Her eyes were as dark as *ebony*.

discern (dih-SERN) recognize; make out clearly
❖ They could not *discern* the difference between the original painting and its copy.

laden (LAYD-uhn) loaded
❖ Tourists are often *laden* with too many suitcases.

waver (WAY-vuhr) flicker; vary in brightness
❖ The light in her window never did *waver*.

ravaged (RAV-ihjd) ruined
❖ My town was *ravaged* by the war.

callused (KAL-uhst) covered with thickened areas of skin
❖ I could tell from her *callused* fingers that she played the guitar.

cascaded (kas-KAY-dihd) fell like a waterfall
❖ Her beautiful long hair *cascaded* down her back.

implored (ihm-PLAWRD) begged
❖ He *implored* me to help him find a place to stay.

lavish (LAV-ihsh) more than is needed; extravagant
❖ No one knew how they could afford such a *lavish* wedding.

The buildings of Chinatown are stoutly constructed of brick, and while some are broad and others thin, they rise no higher than four solid stories. Many contain stained-glass windows decorated with flower and diamond patterns, and others boast balconies with fancy wrought-iron railings.

Only one building stands above the rest. Its turret-like tower is visible even from the harbor, because the cone-shaped roof is made of copper.

In the early days, Chang the merchant tailor owned this building. He used the main floor for his store and rented out the others. But he kept the tower room for his own use, for the sun filled it with light. This was the room where his wife and daughter worked.

His daughter's name was Yenna, and her beauty was beyond compare. She had ivory skin, sparkling eyes, and her hair hung long and silken, shining like polished ebony. All day long she and her mother sat by the tower window and sewed with silver needles and silken threads. They sang songs while they worked, and their voices rose in wondrous harmonies.

In all Chinatown, the craftsmanship of Yenna and her mother was considered the finest. Search as they might, customers could not discern where holes had once pierced their shirts. Buttonholes never stretched out of shape, and seams were all but invisible.

One day, a young man came into the store laden with garments for mending. His shoulders were broad and strong, yet his eyes were soft and caring. Many times he came, and many times he saw Yenna. For hours he would sit and watch her work. They fell deeply in love, though few words were spoken between them.

Spring came and boats bound for the northern gold fields began to sail again. It was time for the young man to go. He had borrowed money to pay his way over to the New World, and now he had to repay his debts. Onto his back he threw his blankets and tools, food and warm jackets. Then he set off with miners from around the world, clutching gold pans and shovels.

Yenna had little to give him in farewell. All she found in the kitchen was a ginger root as large as her hand. As she stroked its brown knobs and bumpy eyes, she whispered to him, "This will warm you in the cold weather. I will wait for you, but, like this piece of ginger, I, too, will age and grow dry." Then she pressed her lips to the ginger, and turned away.

"I will come back," the young man said. "The fire burning for you in my heart can never be extinguished."

Thereafter, Yenna lit a lamp at every nightfall and set it in the tower window. Rains lashed against the glass, snow piled low along the ledge, and ocean winds rattled the frame. But the flame did not waver, even though the young man never sent letters. Yenna did not weep uselessly, but continued to sew and sing with her mother.

There were few unmarried women in Chinatown, and many men came to seek Yenna's hand in marriage. Rich gold miners and sons of successful merchants bowed before her, but she always looked away. They gave her grand gifts, but still she shook her head, until finally the men grew weary and called her crazy. In China, parents arranged all marriages, and daughters became the property of their husbands. But Chang the merchant tailor treasured his daughter's happiness and let her be.

One winter, an epidemic ravaged the city. When it was over, Chang had lost his wife and his eyesight. Yenna led him up to the tower where he could feel the sun and drifting clouds move across his face. She began to sew again, and while she sewed, she sang for her father. The lamp continued to burn steadily at the tower window as she worked. With twice the amount of work to do, she labored long after dusk. She fed the flame more oil and sent her needle skimming through the heavy fabrics. Nimbly her fingers braided shiny cords and coiled them into butterfly buttons. And when the wick sputtered into light each evening, Yenna's heart soared momentarily into her love's memories. Nights passed into weeks, months turned into years, and four years quickly flew by.

One day a dusty traveler came into the store and flung a bundle of ragged clothes onto the counter. Yenna shook out the first shirt, and out rolled a ginger root. Taking it into her hand, she saw that pieces had been nibbled off, but the core of the root was still firm and fragrant.

She looked up. There stood the man she had promised to wait for. His eyes appeared older and wiser.

"Your gift saved my life several times," he said. "The fire of the ginger is powerful indeed."

"Why is the ginger root still firm and heavy?" she wondered. "Should it not have dried and withered?"

"I kept it close to my heart and my sweat coated it. In lonely moments, my tears soaked it." His callused hands reached out for her. "Your face has not changed."

"Nor has my heart," she replied. "I have kept a lamp burning all these years."

"So I have heard," he smiled. "Will you come away with me now? It has taken many years to gather enough gold to buy a farm. I have built you a house on my land."

For the first time since his departure, tears cascaded down Yenna's face. She shook her head. "I cannot leave. My father needs me."

"Please come with me," the young man pleaded. "You will be very happy, I promise."

Yenna swept the wetness from her cheeks. "Stay

with me and work this store instead," she implored.

The young man stiffened and said proudly, "A man does not live in his wife's house." And the eyes that she remembered so well gleamed with determination.

"But this is a new land," she cried. "Must we forever follow the old ways?"

She reached out for him, but he brushed her away. With a curse, he hurled the ginger root into the fireplace. As the flames leaped up, Yenna's eyes blurred. The young man clenched and unclenched his fists in anger. They stood like stone.

At last the man turned to leave, but suddenly he knelt at the fireplace. Yenna saw him reach in with the tongs and pull something out of the flames.

"Look!" he whispered in amazement. "The ginger refuses to be burnt! The flames cannot touch it!"

Yenna looked and saw black burn marks charring the root, but when she took it in her hand, she found it still firm and moist. She held it to her nose, and found the fragrant sharpness still there.

The couple embraced and swore to stay together. They were married at a lavish banquet attended by all of Chinatown. There, the father passed his fingers over his son-in-law's face and nodded in satisfaction.

Shortly after, the merchant Chang died, and the young couple moved away. Yenna sold the business and locked up the tower room. But on nights when boats pull in from far away, they say a flicker of light can still be seen in that high window. And Chinese women are reminded that ginger is one of their best friends.

READING FOR UNDERSTANDING

1. What does the description of the work Yenna and her mother did tell you about the values of this community?

2. Suggest a reason, other than her beauty, why the young man fell in love with Yenna.

3. Why was Yenna seen as unusual by the other Chinese?

4. What does the lamp that Yenna lit every night stand for in this story?

5. What happened to the ginger root while the young man was gone? What happened when he returned?

6. What is the meaning of the ginger root in this story?

RESPONDING TO THE STORY

In this story, objects and items have meanings beyond their everyday uses. Which single item in the story do you think best represents the beliefs of the community? Describe this item and explain its significance.

REVIEWING VOCABULARY

Match each word on the left with the correct definition on the right.

1. ebony
2. discern
3. laden
4. waver
5. ravaged
6. callused
7. cascaded
8. implored
9. lavish

a. loaded
b. begged
c. flicker; vary in brightness
d. fell like a waterfall
e. covered with thickened areas of skin
f. more than is needed; extravagant
g. a hard, black wood
h. recognize; make out clearly
i. ruined

THINKING CRITICALLY ABOUT CULTURE

1. What did you learn from this story about the life of the Chinese in the United States? Compare Chang the tailor's life with that of the young man Yenna loves.

2. In what way did Chang break with the tradition of his culture in his treatment of his daughter?

3. What Chinese traditions were Yenna and her young man unwilling to go against? What did they finally do?

4. The story points out the difficulties of living in a country where the culture is different from your own. If you lived in another culture, are there any traditions you would find difficult to give up? Is there room for compromise? Explain.

HOW THUNDER AND LIGHTNING CAME TO BE

an Eskimo myth

By Ramona Maher

Picture a warm, humid, summer day. Dark clouds are rolling in. Suddenly, lightning flashes through the sky. Then a deep rumble of thunder echoes all around. Some people are frightened, which is not surprising. Lightning storms are one of the ways nature reveals its power.

The Eskimo people, the largest Native American group in Alaska and northern Canada, believed that everything in nature had a spirit. These powerful spirits ruled nature. The Eskimo led hard lives. They had to rely on hunting for food. The caribou, a type of reindeer, provided food, clothing, shelter, and tools. Most Eskimo lived near the sea in order to hunt seal, walrus, whales, and bears.

In the summer months the Eskimo would make camps inland, hunting for fish and birds. When summer storms rolled in, they huddled together in fear and wonder. It was times like these that must have inspired the creation of a myth that explained how thunder and lightning came to be.

VOCABULARY WORDS

deserted (dih-ZER-tuhd) abandoned; not inhabited
❖ At the top of the mountain, we found a *deserted* cabin.

makeshift (MAYK-shihft) temporary; suitable for a short time
❖ The children put together a *makeshift* tree house this summer.

kindle (KIHN-duhl) start a fire
❖ Everyone in camp had to learn how to *kindle* a campfire.

fidgeted (FIHJ-iht-uhd) moved restlessly
❖ The young child *fidgeted* during the movie.

appease (uh-PEEZ) satisfy or relieve
❖ I ate a sandwich to *appease* my hunger.

flourished (FLOOR-ihsht) waved in the air
❖ The soldier *flourished* his sword as he approached.

barbed (BAHRBD) having sharp, curved points
❖ We put up a *barbed* wire fence to keep the sheep inside.

KEY WORDS

auklet (AWK-liht) small, diving shorebird
❖ The *auklet* dove quickly for the shiny fish.

ptarmigan (TAHR-muh-guhn) game bird
❖ We roasted the *ptarmigan* over an open fire.

pyrite (PY-ryt) a yellow mineral (iron sulfide)
❖ *Pyrite* occurs almost everywhere in North America.

Once, in a summer camp by a river in Alaska, lived a boy of twelve and his ten-year-old sister. Their parents had died during the winter, and the boy was trying very hard to catch enough fish and trap enough birds and foxes to feed himself and his sister.

At night, in their small cabin of logs and grass and moss, they ate the berries the sister had picked during the day. If the boy had caught any fish, they had a splendid meal. Usually, however, there was no fish for dinner, because the older men set their fish wheels turning upstream and caught the fish before they reached the boy's net.

On the nights when they had not had enough to eat, the sister would cry.

"Don't cry," her brother always said. "Tomorrow I will catch an auklet and tie it up on a pole. Other auklets will see it fluttering and will come to the pole. We will have ten auklets for food, tomorrow night!"

But the auklets never came, and the boy and his sister had to eat greens or berries. And the greens and berries never filled their stomachs.

The sister would cry again. "How I wish I were a bear! If I were a bear, I would catch three ptarmigan for my dinner."

"I wish I were a seal," her brother would say. "If I were a seal, I would eat my weight in clams!"

They would wrap themselves up more tightly in their stained, stiff, caribou skins and play the game. They each said what animal they wished to be and then said what kind of food they would eat if they were that animal.

Talking about food lessened their hunger, and they could then fall asleep.

One morning the sister and brother awoke. The sister laid aside her sleeping skin. "How quiet it is this morning!"

"Yes," said her brother, after listening for a few minutes. "I don't hear dogs barking or children playing." He put his head outside the cabin door and looked around.

"Sister!" he said, and his face was pale and frightened. "They have all gone away. Every one has gone back to the winter village!"

"Without us?" His sister began to cry.

The camp was deserted. The makeshift summer houses looked like empty shells. The fish wheels had been taken down and moved. The drying poles were empty of needlefish and strips of salmon. The boats that had been turned upside down on the riverbank were gone. And so were all the people who had come to this summer village with the boy and his sister.

"Don't worry," said the boy. "Those people didn't want to be bothered with us, but they don't know we won't be a bother to anyone. I will kill a seal, and we will have seal oil and meat for the winter. And when those people come back next summer, guess whom they will find here?"

He was pretending to tell a joke, so his sister tried to laugh. "Whom will they find here, Brother?"

He pretended to bend over with laughter. "They will be expecting to find two heaps of bones in this cabin. But they will find you and me, noisier and fatter and happier than ever!"

The only thing they had to eat during the next two days was a white owl, which they roasted over a fire of moss and sticks. Because they did not have any seal oil for fuel, it took the sister a long while, rubbing two firestones together, to kindle the moss and sticks. The sister then turned the owl over and over above the fire, using a sharpened, peeled stick for a roasting spit.

The owl made a small, stringy dinner.

"It was mostly feathers," said the girl mournfully after she and her brother had eaten.

The sister wrapped herself up in her hard caribou

skin, and the brother covered himself up with his skin. They watched the tiny fire die.

The girl started the game.

> *"My brother, dear brother,*
> *What kind of animal shall we be?*
> *Shall we turn into wolves?*
> *If we turn into wolves,*
> *We can outrace a squirrel;*
> *We can catch it and eat it and eat it!"*

The brother thought for a moment. "No, not wolves," he said finally.

The sister sighed. After a moment, she said:

> *"My brother, dear brother,*
> *What kind of animal shall we be?*
> *Shall we turn into bears?*
> *If we turn into bears,*
> *We will have sharp teeth.*
> *Sharp teeth for eating! Let us be bears!"*

The brother was silent for a moment. "No, not bears," he said at length.

The sister fidgeted for a moment. She thought of the splintery piece of owl bone on which she had sucked to try to appease her hunger.

> *"Tiny bird bones don't help my big hunger,*
> *My brother, dear brother.*
> *Let us turn into birds.*
> *We won't have to eat much,*
> *And we'll have beautiful feathers!"*

Her brother breathed in and out slowly, as if giving this idea long thought. "No," he sighed gustily, "Not birds."

The game was beginning to help the girl forget her hunger. What could she next suggest they could be?

"My brother, dear brother,
Let's be a fish, a bright silver salmon.
Let's be a cod. We can sleep in the river.
We can eat weeds, and never leave the river,
And never be hungry. Oh, let's be a fish!"

"No," said her brother after a pause. "Not fish."

The girl suggested that they turn into walrus, so they could dine on seafood.

"No," said her brother. "Not walrus. Too ugly, and too wrinkled."

"My brother, dear brother,
Let's turn into caribou!"

"No," said her brother. "Not caribou, either."

The girl thought. What could they be, she wondered, so they could be strong, and never hungry, and not have other animals attempting to eat them?

"Tiny birds' bones don't help my big hunger,
My brother, dear brother.
Shall we be thunder?
Shall we be lightning?
If you were thunder
And I were lightning,
You could go boom,
And I could strike and kill
With my antlers of lightning!"

The girl spoke loudly. "Let us be thunder and lightning!"

"Yes!" said her brother, his voice firm and strong. He leaped off the floor and began to shake the dried, stiff caribou hide until it rattled.

The sister sprang up and found her firestones. She began striking them together, until sparks flew like tiny barbs of light. They went outside, the boy still shaking the dried skin and the girl striking sparks with her firestones. They continued, until the boy was a booming,

muttering noise in the far mountains and the girl was lightning.

Whenever they saw something they wanted to eat, the girl merely flourished her antlers of lightning, thrusting the barbed horns into a bear or a deer or a seal, and they had plenty of food. They were never hungry again.

The sister and brother roamed about the earth, but now and then in the summer, when their people were at the summer camp, they went back. There they caused it to thunder and to lightning and to rain so often that the people decided never again to use this place as a summer village.

The brother and sister are very old now, but they may still be heard: the boy rattling the stiff caribou skin, the girl striking together her pyrite firestones. They visit the earth most often in the summertime.

READING FOR UNDERSTANDING

1. Why were the brother and sister living on their own?
2. Arrange the following incidents in the order in which they occurred:
   (a) The children roasted a white owl for dinner
   (b) The boy rattled his caribou skin, and the girl struck her firestones
   (c) The children awoke and found the camp deserted
   (d) The girl suggested that they become thunder and lightning
   (e) The girl suggested that they become walruses.
3. The children considered becoming a number of animals. In only one case did either give a reason for rejecting an animal. What was the animal, and why did they reject it?
4. Describe how the brother behaved in the story toward his sister.
5. What do you think about the behavior of the people in the summer camp?

RESPONDING TO THE MYTH

The children played a game to keep their minds off their hunger. They asked themselves what they would eat if they were various animals. What other ways might children distract themselves when they are feeling worried or concerned about something?

REVIEWING VOCABULARY

Match the word on the left with the correct definition on the right.

1. deserted
2. makeshift
3. kindle
4. fidgeted
5. appease
6. flourished
7. barbed

a. waved in the air
b. satisfy or relieve
c. temporary; suitable for a short time
d. start a fire
e. abandoned; not inhabited
f. moved restlessly
g. having sharp, curved points

THINKING CRITICALLY

1. Part of being an effective storyteller is holding your audience's attention. Imagine sitting around a fire and listening to this story. When the little sister plays the game, it is presented as a song or a chant. Explain the effect this would have on the audience. Whom would it mainly appeal to?

2. After explaining how thunder and lightning came to be, the story mentioned the abandoned summer camp and why the people decided never to go back there. When you think about the children and what happened to them at the camp, what other message do you think this story is giving to its audience? Is there a lesson about human relationships?

3. Discuss what explanations you were given as a child when you asked about thunder and lightning. How are they similar to or different from the one you read in this story?

A STRANGE SLED RACE
a Hawaiian myth
By Vivian L. Thompson

Hawaii is part of the United States even though it is thousands of miles away in the central Pacific Ocean. The Hawaiian islands were created by volcanoes, many of which are still active today. It is no wonder that Hawaiian mythology has a volcano goddess—the mighty Pele.

What may be surprising is that there is also a goddess of snow—Poliahu. Because of its great height, there is snow year-round on the peak of Mauna Kea on the island of Hawaii. Mauna Kea, which means "white mountain," is also a sleeping volcano. What do you think will happen when the volcano goddess and the goddess of snow come face to face?

VOCABULARY WORDS

maidens (MAYD-nz) young, unmarried women
❖ The *maidens* in the village gathered for the dance.

mantles (MAN-tuhlz) loose, sleeveless capes
❖ She was busy sewing *mantles* for all the soldiers in the school play.

inferior (ihn-FIHR-ee-uhr) low in quality
❖ Sometimes, supermarket items that are cheaper are also *inferior*.

jagged (JAG-ihd) having ragged edges
❖ The stranger had a *jagged* scar across his cheek.

spurted (SPER-tihd) gushed; squirted
❖ He felt faint when the blood *spurted* from his cut.

crest (KREHST) line or surface along the top
❖ When the clouds cleared, we were able to see the *crest* of the mountain.

defy (dih-FY) resist boldly
❖ The brave soldier swore to *defy* the approaching troops.

arc (AHRK) part of a circle
❖ After the heavy rain, the *arc* of a rainbow appeared.

dwindled (DWIHN-duhld) became smaller and smaller
❖ As winter approached, the amount of evening sunlight *dwindled*.

**P**oliahu and her snow maidens one day covered their dazzling snow mantles with mantles of golden sunshine. They took their long, slender sleds to the race course below the snowfields. There a narrow grassy track had been laid, dropping swiftly toward the sea.

High, tinkling laughter filled the air as the maidens urged the goddess to race. Poliahu was very willing. She made a running start, threw herself upon her sled, and plunged down. Far below she came to a stop, marked the spot, and lifted her sled aside.

One after another the snow maidens followed, but none reached the goddess's mark. As they gathered below they discovered a stranger in their midst, a handsome woman dressed in black mantle and robe.

Fixing gleaming black eyes upon the goddess of snow, she spoke. "I should like to race with you, but I have no sled."

"You may use one of ours," Snow Goddess said, and a maiden quickly offered hers.

The stranger took it without a word of thanks. Then she and Poliahu climbed up the mountain slope. The maidens watched from below. The stranger swooped down the slope and flashed past them. There was no doubt she was skillful. Poliahu followed and passed the other's stopping place.

"That sled did not fit me!" said the dark-eyed stranger.

A taller maiden offered her sled. Again the long, slow climb. Again the short, swift descent. Both sleds went farther than before, but Poliahu's still led.

"An inferior sled!" the woman said with scorn.

"We have no inferior sleds," Snow Goddess replied coldly. "Let us race again, and you shall take mine."

"I have always raced on a longer course," said the

woman. "Let us go higher up the mountain. You shall race first this time."

They exchanged sleds and climbed to the snow line. The stranger waited until Poliahu had started down; then she stamped her foot. The earth trembled. A jagged crack split open across the lower part of the racing course.

The snow maidens, watching below, lost sight of their goddess as steam rose from the crack and formed a curtain. They ran up the slope.

For a moment, the steam cleared. They caught a glimpse of Poliahu racing toward the widening crack. The woman in black was close behind her, standing upright on her speeding sled. In horror they saw her black robe turn red and her eyes glow like burning coals. They knew now! She was Pele—Volcano Goddess!

She stamped again. They felt the molten lava come rumbling through underground passages in answer to her signal. It spurted out along the crack.

Swiftly the snow maidens raised their arms toward the snowy peaks and began to chant. The air grew chill as gray Cloud Goddesses gathered to aid Poliahu. They sent snow swirling down from the top of the mountain, hissing as it struck the heated earth. The spurting lava died.

Pele, in a fury, gave a crackling shout. The lava leaped up again, forming a row of fiery fountains directly ahead of Poliahu.

The snow maidens watched fearfully. There was no way that Poliahu could slow her sled nor turn it aside. She plunged through the wall of fire.

Her golden mantle burst into flame. Throwing it off and leaping from her sled, Snow Goddess stood robed in dazzling white. A red-gold river raced toward her from the fire fountains. On its crest rode Pele. Poliahu waited, unmoved.

Volcano Goddess burst through the flames without harm. She sprang from her sled to face the young woman who dared to defy her.

Snow Goddess swung her mantle in a wide arc. A blast of icy wind swept down the mountain. Her silvery hair and dazzling garments streamed out behind her.

Volcano Goddess shivered. The leaping fountains dwindled. The racing river slowed.

She screamed at the lava, "Swallow her up!"

But the lava fountains died. The lava river grew sluggish. Still deadly, it flowed to the very feet of Snow Goddess. She flung her arms wide. The river split in two, leaving her unharmed in the center. It made its way beyond her, moving slowly down to the sea. There it formed a long, flat point of land, known to this day as Leaf-of-Smooth-Lava.

Volcano Goddess stared, unable to believe what she saw. Her red mantle turned black again. Her glowing eyes dulled. Shivering with cold, she disappeared as mysteriously as she had come.

High, tinkling laughter filled the air once more as the snow goddess and her maidens picked up their sleds and returned to their snowy home.

Pele never again crossed over Mauna Kea to Poliahu's side of the island, although she still sent lava pouring down the southern side.

READING FOR UNDERSTANDING

1. What game were the Snow Goddess and her maidens playing?
2. Why did the Snow Goddess and her maidens behave as they did toward the stranger in the black mantle?
3. What did Pele do during the race?
4. Why do you think Pele behaved the way she did?
5. How did Poliahu react to Pele's actions? How did she show that she was a true goddess?
6. This myth describes the opposite forces of fire and ice. What human emotions could these forces represent? How are the goddesses themselves like people?

RESPONDING TO THE MYTH

The two main characters in this myth, Poliahu and Pele, are presented as opposites. Which goddess do you find more interesting? Explain why.

REVIEWING VOCABULARY

The following sentences are based on the myth. Decide which of the words following the sentences best fits each blank. Write your answers on a separate sheet of paper.

1. One day Poliahu and her snow _____ changed their snow _____ to ones of golden sunshine.
2. After the stranger in black lost the race twice, she complained that her sled was _____.
3. Pele stamped her foot and a _____ crack split the earth. When she stamped again, lava _____ out of the crack.

4. As Pele rode the _____ of the lava, Poliahu dared to _____ her by waiting for her. When Poliahu swung her mantle in a wide _____, the fountains of lava froze and _____ in the air.

Words: *arc, crest, defy, dwindled, inferior, jagged, maidens, mantles, spurted*

THINKING CRITICALLY

1. How does the storyteller help build suspense in this story? Use details from the story in your response.
2. The storyteller uses vivid language to tell about the snow goddess and her maidens and the volcano goddess. How do these descriptions of the goddesses remind you of forces in nature?
3. Describe the conflict or problem in the story. When was it clear that there would be a problem for Poliahu? When did the events reach a turning point? What was the final outcome?

Unit 2

STORIES FROM THE CARIBBEAN

ATARIBA AND NIGUAYONA

a legend from the Taino people of Puerto Rico

Adapted by Harriet Rohmer and Jesús Guerrero Rea

Legends are stories that survive from the past because of their great appeal. They usually are based upon real people or events. However, these stories change as they are told from generation to generation. Ordinary people are turned into heroes or heroines of great strength and courage. Events become larger than life.

Legends give you information about the people who tell them. "Atariba and Niguayona" is a legend of the Taino people of Puerto Rico. The Taino were Native Americans. They lived on the Caribbean island of Puerto Rico long before Columbus landed there in 1493. Puerto Rico is now part of the United States.

The Taino were peaceful. They grew cassava roots, they prayed to their god Yucaju, and they respected nature. Their culture was destroyed by the Spanish who came after Columbus.

In this legend, Niguayona goes on a long journey to save his seriously ill friend, Atariba. Will he succeed? Discover what challenges he faces on his journey. As you read, think about what makes this story a legend. Also, think about why Niguayona became a hero of the Taino people.

VOCABULARY WORDS

conch (KAHNGK) large, spiral-shaped shellfish
❖ The girl was thrilled to find a *conch* shell on the beach.

macaw (muh-KAW) South- and Central-American parrot
❖ We saw the *macaw* in the zoo's birdhouse.

alighted (uh-LYT-uhd) landed; settled
❖ The frog jumped from one stone and *alighted* on another.

cassava (kuh-SAH-vuh) plant root
❖ The *cassava* root was a major part of the Taino diet.

comet (KAH-muht) starlike, moving object in the sky
❖ We watched the *comet* leave a trail in the sky.

fiesta (fee-EHS-tuh) festival or celebration
❖ The *fiesta* started with a parade.

KEY WORDS

Taino (tah-EE-noh) a Native American people
❖ The *Taino* people greeted Columbus when he landed in the Caribbean.

bohique (boh-EE-kay) Taino word for healer
❖ The *bohique* helped the Taino when they were sick.

jutias (hoo-TEE-ahs) small, furry animals
❖ The *jutias* were sometimes kept as pets.

caimoni (kai-moh-NEE) tall, tropical tree
❖ The *caimoni* tree grew deep in the forest.

Yucaju (yoo-KAH-hoo) god of the Taino
❖ The Taino people prayed to *Yucaju* for help.

anona (ahn-NOH-nah) large, heart-shaped fruit
❖ The *anona* fruit lay on the floor of the forest.

 **L**ittle **Atariba** [ah-tah-REE-bah], with her long black hair and eyes like seashells, was very sick. She lay in a hammock in the hut of the *bohique*, the village healer. But the bohique could not cure her.

Her best friend, Niguayona [nee-gwah-YOH-nah], watched her sadly. He remembered how happy he had been, wandering with Atariba by the riverbank. Together they had played with the parrots and the furry *jutías*. Only days before he had made her a beautiful necklace of seashells and green stones.

Time passed and Atariba still did not recover. Niguayona wandered alone along the riverbank, playing his conch-shell horn. "How can Atariba be cured?" he wondered.

One afternoon, a golden-green macaw alighted on Niguayona's shoulder.

"On the far side of the forest grows a tall *caimoni* tree," said the bird. "Pick the fruit of this tree, place it on the lips of your Atariba, and she will be cured." And having spoken, the golden-green macaw flew off into the forest.

Niguayona ran toward the village. After hearing his story, his mother and father agreed that he must try to find the tall *caimoni* tree. The *bohique* began to pray for him.

Niguayona entered the forest alone, but he was not afraid. The tree frogs sang to him. An owl called out. Night came quickly and it was soon quite dark. He sat down to rest beneath a large tree and ate a small piece of the cassava cake his mother had given him. Then he said a prayer to Yucaju, the great god of the Taino people.

"Yucaju, dweller of heaven, grant that I may soon find the tall *caimoni* tree!"

The next day as he walked through the forest, Niguayona found a beautiful *anona* fruit lying under a

pile of leaves.

"How delicious it looks!" he thought. But he did not eat it. Instead, he placed it carefully in his bag. "If I don't find the *caimoni* fruit, perhaps I could touch the *anona* to Atariba's lips."

Another day passed, and Niguayona still did not find the *caimoni* tree. He was becoming very tired. The forest thorns tore his skin. The cassava cake was all gone, and he was hungry.

He walked on until he came to a wide, deep river, which blocked his way. Thinking of Atariba, he sat down on the riverbank and began to cry. "How can I find the *caimoni* now?" he asked himself.

After a while Niguayona bravely dried his tears. Then he saw a shining light beside him. It was the *anona*. "I will light your path from the sky," she said.

The *anona* rose high above the treetops and shone over the entire forest. Higher and higher she rose until she became a majestic comet in the sky.

Then the river spoke to Niguayona. "Leap on my back," said the river. And the boy leaped on the river's back and sailed across the wide, deep water as a canoe moves, faster than the wind.

When Niguayona landed on the far side of the river, he ran toward the tall *caimoni* tree that was growing on the edge of the forest. He climbed to the top of the tree and plucked a red fruit from the highest branch. Then he mounted the smiling water once again and was carried quickly to the very riverbank where he had once walked with Atariba.

The people of the village were waiting for Niguayona. Day and night they had prayed to the great god Yucaju for his safe return. They had eaten nothing since his departure so that their prayers might have more power.

"Hurry, Niguayona!" they cried. "Atariba is dying!"

Niguayona raced to the village and breathlessly approached Atariba's still body. He touched the fruit to her lips, which were burning with fever.

For a moment, nothing happened. Then life began to return to Atariba's little body. She moaned and opened her eyes. Slowly she sat up and looked around her.

"The *caimoni* must contain the blood of the gods," whispered the people.

After Atariba recovered, there was a fiesta with many songs and dances in praise of the gods. And once again Atariba and Niguayona wandered together along the riverbank.

With the passing of time, Atariba and Niguayona became strong and compassionate leaders of the Taino people of Puerto Rico. Their story is remembered to this day.

READING FOR UNDERSTANDING

1. Arrange the following incidents in the order in which they occurred:

   (a) Niguayona realized how much he needed Atariba.

   (b) Atariba recovered.

   (c) The *bohique* could not cure Atariba.

   (d) Niguayona dried his tears and decided to be brave.

   (e) Niguayona's parents listened to his plans to find the *caimoni* tree.

2. How did Niguayona learn about the healing power of the *caimoni* tree?

3. Why didn't he eat the *anona* fruit? Give evidence from the story that tells you why.

4. Why did Niguayona pray to Yucaju?

5. Why do you think Niguayona did not give up on finding the *caimoni* tree?

6. How do you think the Taino people felt about Niguayona?

7. Why did the Taino people believe that the *caimoni* fruit would cure illness?

RESPONDING TO THE LEGEND

At the end of the legend, we learn that "Atariba and Niguayona became strong and compassionate leaders. . ." What traits do they show in the story that tell you they will be good leaders? Write a journal entry describing what you think Atariba and Niguayona were like as leaders.

REVIEWING VOCABULARY

The following sentences are based on the legend.
Decide which of the words following the sentences best
fits each blank. Write your answers on a separate sheet
of paper.

1. Niguayona played a horn made of _____ shell.
2. Suddenly, a golden-green _____ appeared.
3. It _____ on his shoulder.
4. Niguayona's mother had baked him a _____
cake to eat on his journey.
5. The *anona* turned into a _____ in the sky.
6. The people held a _____ to praise the gods.

Words: *comet, cassava, alighted, fiesta, conch, macaw*

THINKING CRITICALLY ABOUT CULTURE

1. A legend tells the story of a hero. The Taino people
told a legend about Niguayona. What makes him a
hero? Give details from the story to support your
answer.
2. Nature plays an important role in this legend. How
do you think the Taino felt about animals, plants,
and rivers? How does this legend show these feelings? Use details from the story in your response.
3. The Taino had a strong sense of community. They
helped and supported one another. How did the
Taino help and support Niguayona? What examples
in the legend show this?

PEDRO ANIMALA AND THE CARRAO BIRD

a Puerto Rican folktale

By Pura Belpré

Pura Belpré, the author of this folktale, was a born storyteller. In fact, she came from a family of storytellers. As a child in Puerto Rico, she listened eagerly to the folktales told to her by her father and grandmother. As an adult, she moved to New York City and became a librarian. She began telling and writing down the stories she heard as a child. Soon Pura Belpré became well known for her folktales from Puerto Rico.

Although it is located in the Caribbean, the island of Puerto Rico is part of the United States. The Spanish influence has remained strong there ever since Columbus claimed Puerto Rico for Spain in 1493. Spanish is the main language spoken there, and the Puerto Rican people still like to tell the old Spanish folktales. Some of their favorite stories are about a character named Pedro Animala.

Have you ever played a trick on someone? Has anyone ever fooled you? In "Pedro Animala and the Carrao Bird," we meet Pedro, a trickster. The trickster is a common figure in folktales. He takes advantage of others by fooling them. In this tale, he teaches a woman a lesson she'll never forget. How does she fall into his trap? Read to find out.

VOCABULARY WORDS

wits (WIHTS) cleverness
* ❖ "In a dangerous world, one has to live by one's *wits*."

ajar slightly open
* ❖ The parents left the bedroom door *ajar* so they could hear the baby cry.

papaya (puh-PEYE-uh) yellow tropical fruit
* ❖ She enjoyed the taste of the juicy *papaya*.

soothsayer (SOOTH-say-uhr) someone who interprets the past or predicts the future
* ❖ Does anyone still ask a *soothsayer* for advice?

cocked (KAHKT) tilted to one side
* ❖ The dog *cocked* his head when the girl spoke to him.

foretell (fawr-TEHL) tell about the future
* ❖ The woman claimed that she could *foretell* a flood.

sheepishly (SHEEP-ihsh-lee) meekly, stupidly
* ❖ He *sheepishly* admitted that he made a silly mistake.

vow (VOW) a serious promise
* ❖ As she left her homeland, she made a *vow* to return.

KEY WORDS

carrao bird (kah-RAH-oh) black tropical bird with long legs and a long, curving bill
* ❖ The *carrao bird* lives in the highlands of Puerto Rico.

buenos días (BWEH-nohs DEE-ahs) Spanish for "good morning"
* ❖ "*Buenos días,*" said the friends to one another when they met.

pesetas (puh-SAY-tuhz) Spanish money
* ❖ Dollars have replaced *pesetas* in modern Puerto Rico.

Long, long ago there lived in the high-lands a man called Pedro Animala. He was known to live by his wits, for the word "work" was missing from his vocabulary.

One day he went hunting and caught a young carrao bird. He decided to go to town and sell it. But on his way to town he passed a house with its door ajar. He peeped inside. A woman was filling a glass jar with slices of papaya candy and talking to herself.

"Now that I have finished, I will put the jar in the cupboard," she said. "We shall have dinner as soon as my husband returns from shopping. Then I will surprise him with the papaya candy."

Pedro Animala laughed to himself. Why walk all the way to town when here was a buyer just made to order?

He knocked at the door. The woman came to answer.

"*Buenos días*," said Pedro Animala.

"*Buenos días*," replied the woman.

"How would you like to buy a soothsayer bird?" asked Pedro Animala.

"A soothsayer bird? I have never seen or heard of one!" said the woman.

"Well, you are looking at one now. Would you like to buy it?"

"I would if you give me a demonstration."

Pedro tapped the bird's head lightly. "Carrao, carrao!" cried the bird.

"What did he say?" asked the woman.

"That you have put a jar filled with papaya candy in the cupboard."

"Why, that is true!" said the woman. "Make him say something else."

Pedro Animala tapped the bird's head again. "Carrao, carrao!" cried the bird once more.

"What does he say now?" asked the woman excitedly.

"That you are waiting to have dinner when your husband returns from shopping. Then you will surprise him with the papaya candy."

"Marvelous!" cried the woman. "Yes, yes, I will buy your soothsayer bird! How much do you want for it?"

"Fifty pesetas."

"Fifty pesetas shall it be!" said the woman.

She gave him the money and took the bird, and Pedro Animala went on his way.

He was no sooner gone than the woman tapped the bird gently on the head. "Carrao, carrao!" cried the bird.

The woman cocked her head and waited. The bird said nothing else.

So she tapped his head once more. "Carrao, carrao!" the bird cried quickly.

She was about to tap the bird's head again when the door opened and her husband came in.

"What in the world are you doing with that bird?"

he asked.

"I am trying to make him foretell something," she said. "This is a soothsayer bird!"

"A soothsayer bird? Woman, that is a carrao bird! Tap his head and you will hear him cry his name. Go ahead! Do it!"

But his wife knew better than to tap the bird's head again.

"Where did you get it?" asked her husband.

"I bought it for fifty pesetas," she replied sheepishly.

To her surprise her husband began to laugh. "If I hadn't just seen Pedro Animala making merry in town, I would vow he had been here. That's just the sort of thing he is famous for."

To that his wife said never a word. She promised herself that the next time Pedro Animala came by, she would even things with him. But she never did, for Pedro Animala never calls twice at the same place.

READING FOR UNDERSTANDING

1. Arrange the following incidents in the order in which they occurred:
   (a) The woman's husband figured out where she got the bird.
   (b) Pedro Animala went hunting.
   (c) The woman paid for the bird.
   (d) Pedro Animala saw the woman filling the candy jar.
   (e) Pedro Animala made the bird answer.
2. What made Pedro decide not to sell his bird in town?
3. How did Pedro gain the woman's trust?
4. What did the woman overlook when she agreed to buy the bird? Explain.
5. Without being told, how did the woman's husband know who sold her the bird?
6. What reason, other than money, did Pedro have for selling the bird to the woman?

RESPONDING TO THE FOLKTALE

Have you or someone you know ever played "the trick-ster"? Has anyone ever played a harmless trick on you? Describe what happened, and tell how you felt. Why might someone want to avoid being tricked?

REVIEWING VOCABULARY

The following sentences are based on the folktale. Decide which of the words following the sentences best fits each blank. Write your answers on a separate sheet of paper.

1. Pedro Animala was a man who lived by his
   _____.
2. Pedro Animala noticed a house with the door
   _____.

3. A woman was putting candy made of _____ into a jar.
4. Pedro told her that the bird was a _____.
5. The woman _____ her head as she waited.
6. She told her husband that the bird could _____ things.
7. Then she _____ told him how much she paid for the bird.
8. The husband said that if he hadn't already seen Pedro in town, he would _____ that Pedro had been in their home.

Words: *vow, cocked, papaya, sheepishly, wits, soothsayer, foretell, ajar*

THINKING CRITICALLY

1. At the end of the tale, the woman's husband told her to tap the bird's head. Why didn't she do it?
2. The woman didn't tell her husband that Pedro had been there. Why did she keep that a secret?
3. At the end of the tale, the woman promised to "even things" with Pedro Animala. What does this mean? How do you think she might do this?
4. The trickster is a favorite figure in folktales. Why do you think that people enjoy stories about tricksters?

A VERY HAPPY DONKEY
a Haitian folktale
Retold by Diane Wolkstein

Unlike myths, folktales focus on simple characters who demonstrate a special trait. If the trait is a positive one, such as beauty or intelligence, the character usually comes out on top. Characters with undesirable traits, such as stinginess, are usually punished. The stories are meant to entertain as well as to teach a lesson about human nature.

Diane Wolkstein is a well-known storyteller. She gathers and retells stories from around the world. This tale is from Haiti, which is on an island in the West Indies. French is spoken in Haiti, whereas English or Spanish is spoken in most other Caribbean nations. The country is very poor, and Haitians take the growing and selling of food crops very seriously. They manage to find some humorous affection, however, for a farm boy who doesn't take carrots, turnips, and cauliflowers too seriously. See if you can learn what Tiroro, the boy who takes the family donkey to market, learns the hard way!

VOCABULARY WORDS

wastrel (WAYS-truhl) a person who wastes things
❖ When he threw out the leftover food, his friend called him a *wastrel*.

vagabond (VAG-uh-bahnd) an idle wanderer
❖ The *vagabond* wandered from town to town.

turnip (TER-nihp) a plant with a round, light-colored root that is used as a vegetable
❖ She added a raw *turnip* root to her salad.

cauliflower (KAWL-uh-flow-er) a kind of cabbage with a head of white, fleshy, flower clusters.
❖ Cabbage and *cauliflower* are my favorite vegetables.

braying (BRAY-ihng) making a loud, harsh sound like a donkey
❖ When the donkey started *braying*, it scared the baby.

desperation (dehs-puh-RAY-shuhn) reckless readiness to try anything
❖ In *desperation*, she ran after the taxi to try to stop it.

stake (STAYK) a stick or post with a pointed end for driving into the ground
❖ She tied the horse to the *stake* and went into the farmhouse.

KEY WORDS

maïs moulu (mah-EES moo-LOO) [French for "ground corn"] a dish made from flavored ground corn.
❖ The Haitians put honey in their *maïs moulu*.

munched (MUNCHT) chewed steadily, often with a crunching sound
❖ They *munched* on the popcorn throughout the movie.

There was once a woman named Tiyaya and she had a son named Tiroro and a donkey named Banda. She lived in the mountains in a small hut with one door, one window, one table, one chair, and one mat. Her only son, Tiroro, was a wastrel and a vagabond. He never helped his mother, even with the gardening, but spent his days and nights playing the drum.

One morning Tiyaya woke up and said she was sick. "Tiroro, I am so tired I cannot move. You must go to market for me today. Eat your breakfast and go saddle Banda."

Tiroro finished his breakfast of maïs moulu and went to find Banda. Banda was nibbling grass under a tree.

"Come now, Banda," Tiroro said.

"HEE-*huh*. Where are we going?" Banda asked.

"To market," Tiroro answered, leading her back to the house.

Then he saddled Banda and tied two large baskets to the saddle. One he filled with fresh carrots and the other with fresh turnips and cauliflower.

"Tiroro," his mother called to him from the house.

"Yes, Mama."

"Have you the carrots?"

"Yes, Mama."

"And the turnips?"

"Yes, Mama."

"And the cauliflower?"

"Yes, Mama. I've everything. Everything. We're leaving now, Mama."

"And Banda, did you take food for Banda?"

"Yes, Mama. I've everything."

"Then may Papa God go with you. . . . And get a good price for the vegetables."

Tiroro and Banda walked along the mountain path and soon came across other peasants on their way to market. As they walked they told stories and sang and joked and the time went by quickly.

When they reached Pétionville the sun was setting. The others stopped to rest for a few hours. Tiroro decided to do the same. The others unsaddled their donkeys. Tiroro unsaddled Banda. He brought her water in a pail and tied her rope to a stake in the earth. Then he ate a few carrots and lay down to sleep with his head on the baskets.

It seemed to Tiroro that he had just closed his eyes when he heard Banda braying: "HEE-*huh*! HEE-*huh*! HEE-*huh*!"

"What is it, Banda?" Tiroro whispered. "Are you hungry?" He reached his hand into the basket and took out two cauliflowers and brought them to Banda. Banda munched peacefully on the cauliflowers and Tiroro lay down again.

A half hour passed, then: "HEE-*huh*! HEE-*huh*!"

"Again!" Tiroro said, waking up. "You're still hungry?" He reached into the basket and brought out a bundle of turnips and walked over to Banda. Banda munched on the turnips and Tiroro lay down.

But ten minutes later: "HEE-*huh*! HEE-*huh*!"

"Banda, let me sleep!"

"HEE-*huh*! HEE-*huh*! HEE-*huh*! HEE-*huh*!"

"Carrots! Maybe that's what you want!" Tiroro said. And he took two bundles of carrots from the other basket and brought them to Banda. But now that Banda had tasted all the vegetables she was hungrier than ever:

"HEE-*huh*! HEE-*huh*! HEE-*huh*! HEE-*huh*!"

Banda brayed so loudly that the man sleeping next to Tiroro shouted: "Shut that donkey up!"

"What shall I do with you?" Tiroro cried. He was so sleepy and tired. In desperation he went and brought both baskets of vegetables and placed them by the stake in front of Banda. "Now eat and let me sleep!" he said.

A few hours later Tiroro woke up. The peasants were

saddling their donkeys. Tiroro saddled Banda. He picked up the baskets. Oh-oh. . . . Oh-oh. The baskets were empty. There was nothing in them. Banda had eaten every carrot, every turnip, and every bit of cauliflower during the night.

The son of Tiyaya burst into tears. "In the name of Papa God, what shall I do? Someone answer me! What shall I do?"

Papa God answered Tiroro. He said: *"Next time feed your donkey grass."*

Poor Tiroro. He cried and cried. The others continued on their way to market. What was Tiroro to do? He turned up the mountain path toward his home, with an empty stomach, two empty baskets, and a *very* happy donkey.

"HEE-*huh*! HEE-*huh*! HEE-*huh*!"

Banda!

READING FOR UNDERSTANDING

1. How did Tiroro like to spend his days and nights?
2. Why do you think Tiroro's mother wanted him to go to market?
3. Why do you think it was important to get a good price for the vegetables?
4. Did Tiroro know how to take care of the donkey? What actions show this?
5. In what way was the donkey's behavior humanlike?
6. How do you think Tiroro felt when he discovered the empty baskets?
7. How do you think Tiroro's mother reacted when he told her what happened?

RESPONDING TO THE STORY

What kind of person is Tiroro? Would you like to have him as a friend? Why? Why not? Use evidence from the story or from your own experiences in your response.

REVIEWING VOCABULARY

Match each word on the left with the correct definition on the right.

1. wastrel
2. vagabond
3. turnip
4. cauliflower
5. munched
6. stake
7. braying
8. desperation

a. plant with a root that is used as a vegetable
b. person who wastes things
c. kind of cabbage with a white, fleshy head
d. making a loud, harsh sound like a donkey
e. reckless readiness to try anything
f. idle wanderer
g. stick or post with a pointed end for driving into the ground
h. chewed steadily

THINKING CRITICALLY

1. Folktales often teach lessons about human nature. After reading about Tiroro, what lesson did you learn about people's character flaws and weaknesses? Do you think Tiroro changed his ways? Why or why not?
2. What does this tale tell you about Haitian people's feelings and ideas about their god? How did Papa God respond to Tiroro? What did that show about Papa God's relationship with his worshippers?
3. Do you think "A Very Happy Donkey" is a good title for this tale? Why or why not? What other title would be good? Explain.

THE LITTLE GREEN FROG
a tale from the Dominican Republic
Translated by Mary Hanson

Did you ever hear a story that was so wonderful that you felt you had to tell it to someone else? Did you add personal touches that changed it? The following story from the Dominican Republic is just such a story.

This story is a story within a story. The focus on the destruction of the environment tells you it is a modern retelling. Imaginative details have been added to an ancient Indian story to stir wonder and fear.

The children who hear this magical story are Patricia, her brother Ico, and her friend Tero. They are amazed to hear the story told by a little green frog. As you read, try to figure out what makes it such an entertaining story and why people continue to tell it.

VOCABULARY WORDS

massive (MAS-ihv) huge
❖ The men couldn't move the *massive* rock.

jolted (JOHL-tihd) shook up
❖ The car *jolted* us when it came to a sudden stop.

ashy (ASH-ee) of ash color; pale
❖ He looked so *ashy* that I wondered if he was ill.

gruff (GRUF) bad-tempered
❖ He never visited his *gruff* uncle.

chatterbox (CHAT-uhr-bahks) person who never stops talking
❖ She is such a *chatterbox* that she gives me a headache.

astounded (uh-STOWN-dihd) amazed
❖ The magician *astounded* us with his tricks.

tap (TAP) faucet
❖ She went to the *tap* to get a glass of water.

swallow (SWAHL-oh) small bird with long, pointed wings and a forked tail
❖ We saw a *swallow* eating some insects.

grubs (GRUBZ) wormlike larvae of certain insects
❖ The frogs found insects and *grubs* in the pond.

KEY WORD

china (CHEYE-nuh) porcelain or ceramic
❖ We could not use the *china* saucer for the cat's milk.

Patricia thought that the stories the Indians told were very silly—stories like the one that said children could be turned into little frogs if their mothers leave them. They have fathers to look after them, don't they? she thought. And she saw lots of children with no mother out on the streets, begging. And they never got turned into frogs, did they?

On the way back from school she told Tero what she thought about the Indians' stories. Tero was her best friend. He wanted to talk about other things, but Patricia wouldn't leave the matter alone.

"Can you imagine? Stories like the sun and the moon coming out of a cave, or stuff like all men and women coming out of a cave as well, and that one about the sea where—"

"Oh, forget it, Patricia," said Tero, "I'm hungry, and it doesn't really matter anyway."

Tero turned off into his house, and Patricia walked on. When she was standing by the side of the road, waiting to cross, a huge truck roared by. It was loaded with trees, massive trunks just cut down from the forest. Some of them still had branches and leaves on them. As it passed Patricia, the back wheels of the truck hit a pothole and jolted its load. A soft green thing fell from a branch, almost onto her feet. Patricia jumped. She took a step back and then, slowly, she moved closer to see what had fallen off the truck—it was a little green frog.

She stared at it. There it sat, a dull, ashy green color. She could see its bones through the green skin, and its eyes were half-closed. It sat very still, and close to the ground. It was still breathing, but Patricia saw that it wouldn't last long out here where it could be crushed and where the sun would dry it out.

She bent down to pick it up but stopped sharply. A voice seemed to come from the frog saying, "Oh dear, oh dear."

Patricia stood up again and started to run off, but then she stopped. She thought, this is silly, frogs can't talk, but . . . but I heard it. She crouched down again and reached out her hand.

"Don't touch me. Don't kill me," said the frog.

Before she knew it, Patricia was talking back.

"Why can't I touch you?"

"Don't kill me," said the frog.

"I'm not going to kill you," said Patricia. "I only want to move you to a cool place and keep you from being squashed."

The little frog lifted its head up and opened its eyes more. It had greenish yellow eyes with beautiful spots that changed color in the light.

"Well, all right," said the frog. "Thank you."

Patricia looked for a cool place by the side of the road but could not see one. Then she had her idea. She'd take it and put it on the grass that grew at the side of her house. She only hoped that her uncle who lived in her house did not see it because he was a gruff, moody sort of person and might tell her off and throw the little frog onto the road.

So, when she got back to the house, she put the little frog on the cool grass next to one of the walls. Then very quietly, she said, "I'll be back, don't move."

She went into the house, trying to act as if nothing had happened. But there was nobody at home except her older brother Ico. He hadn't gone to school that day because of a cold. She thought of telling him about the little frog but held back. He was too much of a chatterbox to keep such a secret.

She felt she had to tell someone about what she had found, but who? Her uncle? No way! Isabelita, who looked after Ico and her when her parents were away? No, she would think it was black magic. Tero? Maybe.

Patricia went into the kitchen. There was some food

for her on the table, but she wasn't hungry. Hungry? The little green frog must be hungry . . . and thirsty. She could take her dinner to the frog, but then—what do frogs eat?

Patricia jumped. She was talking to herself and didn't see Ico come in.

"What did you say?" he said.

"Nothing," Patricia said.

But she needed to tell him. Perhaps she *could* trust Ico with her secret, even though he was a chatterbox.

"Ico?"

"Mmm."

"What do frogs eat?"

"Why do you ask?" said Ico.

"No, no nothing."

The silence made Patricia tell him.

"Look, Ico, I found a little green frog that talks, out on the road. It fell off a truck right at my feet," she said all in a rush.

Ico looked at her, astounded. He knew that his sister liked to make things up sometimes, but this time she looked so serious.

"Come and see," she said.

Patricia took Ico out of the house to the cool grass by the wall. The little green frog was still there. It looked as if it were asleep.

"Look," said Patricia.

"Tell it to talk," said Ico.

"No, it's asleep. Let's get it some food for when it wakes up."

"No," said the frog.

Ico's eyes nearly popped out. He was going to run away, but Patricia grabbed him by the shirt.

"Wait!" she said.

Ico didn't say a word.

"Don't bother with the food," said the frog. "Just bring me some water. I'm thirsty."

"Get some water," said Patricia to Ico. But he was so frightened he couldn't move. Patricia had to go to the tap herself.

"Don't be afraid," said the frog to Ico. "After I've had a drink, I'll tell you my story."

Patricia brought some water in a little china saucer. The little frog drank slowly. Its skin came back to life and looked much brighter and greener. The children could see that it was feeling better.

"Let's take it indoors," said Ico. Patricia and the frog agreed. They put it on a cotton cloth on the table next to the goldfish, who swam back and forth in a glass bowl. The frog was about to start telling its story when Patricia asked it to wait just a little longer. She wanted her friend Tero to hear the story too, and she ran off and got him. All was ready for the frog to begin:

Hundreds of years ago, the first men and women on this island lived in two caves. One cave was called Cacibajagua. The people in that cave, my people, only came out at night. They were afraid of the sun because they thought it would turn them into trees, stones, or animals.

One night the chief sent his brother out to catch fish, but he didn't get back to the cave in time. He was surprised by the sun and turned into a swallow. The chief was so upset that he left cave Cacibajagua. He took all the women and children with him to the bank of a big river. Then he made the mothers leave their children on the river bank. The children cried out, 'Toa, toa,' which is what children call their mothers in our language.

Morning came, and when the sun rose, it turned all the children into frogs. There they sat, crying helplessly. Then the spirit of the water rose out of the river, her body as clear as glass. The frogs told her what had happened, and she felt sorry for them. She said, "I cannot change what has happened to you, but I can ask the great god-

dess to let you go back to Cacibajagua when you die. As
long as you die a natural death, you will turn back into
children and live in the cave for the rest of time."

The little frogs thanked the water spirit.

Before they left, she gave them each a long, thin
gold medal, the kind our people used to wear on their
foreheads. 'Each of you must have one of these with
you when you die,' she said; 'otherwise you won't turn
back into children.' And the water spirit disappeared
into the river.

The frogs put the medals in their mouths and made
their way up the great river to one of the little streams
that flowed into it. There they found a nice cool place,
where there was lots of food, since from now on they
would have to eat insects and grubs.

Many years passed. The frogs saw the people of the
island working together like brothers and sisters, without harming nature, only taking what they needed to
live; fruit from the trees, fish from the river, and what
animals they needed but no more. And when the frogs
died a natural death, they went back to cave Cacibajagua
and turned into children.

But one day, other people came to the island. They got
rid of the peaceful people, and in no time at all they
began to damage the forest and the rivers and the animals. The sons and daughters of the first little frogs
found it more and more difficult to find good places to
live, and they began to move away. The world was chang-
ing, and they felt that the rain gods had abandoned them.

(The little green frog paused. He looked tired now,
but sipped some water and carried on.)

The last of my people lived in a little pine forest that
was cool and green. But a few days ago the men and
machines came and chopped down all the trees. A lot
of my brothers and sisters were squashed and died and
could not get back to Cacibajagua. Maybe there were
others who have been saved like me. But without water

they will die of thirst and that is not a natural death. They won't be able to return to the cave—and you know what that means: no more children.

A greenish light began to surround the little frog. The light spread until it filled the whole room. Suddenly the little green frog opened its eyes very wide and shouted happily like a child, 'Toa!'

The light made the three children sleepy. They fell back on the bed where they had been sitting, listening. They didn't see the little green frog turn into a naked short-haired boy and disappear."

Isabelita came into the room and turned on the light.

"Ico, Patricia, come and have your tea. Tero! You're here? Your mother is looking for you everywhere."

The three of them looked at each other, puzzled. Then, almost at the same time, they rushed to the table. Beto was waving his colored fins around. Beside the fish bowl was a white cotton cloth and on it, a little flat golden thing—the little green frog's medal.

READING FOR UNDERSTANDING

1. How would you describe Patricia's attitude toward Indian folktales?
2. When Patricia first spoke to the frog, we reached a turning point in the story. Why?
3. How did Ico react to the frog at first? When did his reaction change?
4. What did the water spirit promise the frogs if they died a natural death?
5. Why did the water spirit place such value on dying a natural death?
6. Judging from the present-day context of the story, suggest who the "other people" were who came to the island.
7. What can we assume happened to the frog at the end of the story?
8. Was the frog's story true? What evidence was there to prove this?

RESPONDING TO THE STORY

Imagine that the children told the grown-ups what happened. How do you think the uncle and Isabelita reacted to their story? Write a dialogue that continues the story.

REVIEWING VOCABULARY

Match each word on the left with the correct definition on the right.

1. massive	**a.** amazed	
2. jolted	**b.** wormlike larvae of insects	
3. ashy	**c.** huge	
4. gruff	**d.** shook up	
5. chatterbox	**e.** bad-tempered	
6. astounded	**f.** person who never stops talking	
7. tap		
8. swallow	**g.** of ashy color; pale	
9. grubs	**h.** small bird	
	i. faucet	

THINKING CRITICALLY

1. Do you think Patricia's thoughts about the Indian's stories changed after learning the frog's story? Why or why not?

2. Do you think this folktale was entertaining? Use examples from the story to support your opinion.

3. Do you think the end of the story was clear? Why or why not? If not, describe an ending to the story that you think might be better.

4. This story combines fantasy elements with serious lessons. Do you think this is a good idea? State your opinion about this question and then support it with details from the story.

5. The person who told this story used many devices found in folktales. Name two that you think were effective, and explain why.

Unit 3
STORIES FROM CENTRAL AMERICA

DOOMED LOVERS
an Aztec myth
Retold by Ben Sonder

The Aztec empire thrived in Mexico during the fifteenth century. The Aztec were able to control large areas because of their skilled, well-equipped warriors.

At the time, the Aztec had the most advanced civilization in North America. When the Aztec invaded a region, they took it over and adopted its culture. To the knowledge they gained from the Maya, Toltec, and Zapotec peoples, they brought their own talents for architecture and sculpture. The Aztec empire fell to the Spaniards under Hernando Cortez, who conquered it in 1521.

Today, Mexico City stands on what used to be the capital of the Aztec empire—Tenochtitlán. From the streets of the bustling city, you can see a pair of volcanoes—Popocatepetl and Ixtacihuatl.

This tale attempts to explain the origins of these two volcanoes. It uses the explosive qualities of nature to mirror the passion and intensity of two doomed lovers. The lovers are Popocatepetl, the greatest Aztec warrior, and Ixtacihuatl, the royal princess. Read on to see what other strong emotions are let go during a chain of events set into motion by an ailing emperor.

VOCABULARY WORDS

obsidian (uhb-SIHD-ih-uhn) hard, dark volcanic glass
❖ He studied the unusual rock and said it was *obsidian*.

javelins (JAV-uh-lihnz) light spears for throwing
❖ When the lion came into view, the hunters threw their *javelins*.

brine (BRYN) very salty water
❖ The pickles were stored in a barrel of *brine*.

wary (WAIR-ee) cautious; on one's guard
❖ Even though the owner said the large dog was friendly, I was *wary*.

cease (SEES) to bring or come to an end; stop
❖ After this summer, the concerts in the park will *cease*.

pursuit (per-SOOT) the act of chasing in order to catch or kill
❖ The police were running in *pursuit* of the thief.

betrayed (bee-TRAYD) delivered to the enemy; deceived
❖ He was *betrayed* when his brother told the police where he was hiding.

vowed (VOWD) made a resolution to do something
❖ She *vowed* that she would find a better job.

wafts (WAHFTS) travels gently through the air or over water
❖ Her perfume *wafts* through the house when she visits.

tribute (TRIHB-yoot) something that shows praise
❖ As a *tribute* to their generosity, a party was held in their honor.

 **Thousands of years ago,** a fierce and powerful Aztec emperor lived in the Valley of Mexico near a huge, sparkling lake called Texcoco. His kingdom was one of green splendor and bright skies. It was build along the shores of the lake and bordered by mountains. The kingdom was called Tenochtitlán.

Enemy tribes lived in and around these mountains. Their only thought was to defeat the wealthy kingdom of Tenochtitlán. To defend his people, the emperor had trained his warriors in the latest methods of battle. They knew how to wage war with razor-sharp obsidian hatchet blades. They could hurl pointed javelins at their enemies by using specially designed springboards.

It was hard to kill the warriors of Tenochtitlán. They wore armor made of cotton soaked in brine. The brine hardened the cotton. It was almost impossible to penetrate a warrior's armor with blades or spears.

In the kingdom of Tenochtitlán, no warrior was more fearless and more beloved than Popocatepetl. He was tall and strong and had enormous courage. Yet he could also be gentle and caring.

Despite Popocatepetl's magnificent qualities, the emperor was wary of him. This was because Popocatepetl was in love with the emperor's daughter, Ixtacihuatl. He wanted to marry her, and she was deeply in love with him. The emperor, however, was against the marriage.

Ixtacihuatl was the only child of the emperor. She was as beautiful as she was intelligent. It was obvious to the entire court that the emperor trusted her more than he did his own wife. He had decided long ago that no one but Ixtacihuatl would rule after he was dead.

While she was still a teenager, her father began training her to be ruler. He saw that she had great energy and a sense of humor. She could also be serious and tireless when there was important work to be done. Her talents for ruling became clear.

The emperor did not want anyone to share the throne with his daughter after he died. He soon grew obsessed by this idea. That was why he was against her marrying anyone.

There were many who questioned the emperor's desire that his daughter not marry. Yet, no one was as unhappy about it as Ixtacihuatl. For her, Popocatepetl was everything her heart desired. Her one dream was to marry him and remain with him the rest of her life. She was convinced that he could help her rule the kingdom. The fact that her father would not trust him made her doubt his abilities as emperor.

Indeed, her father's age made him less and less capable as a ruler. He was growing weak and ill. He put all his energy into training his daughter to rule Tenochtitlán as he saw fit. He let go of his duties as emperor and focused on this one project.

Word spread about the failing health of the emperor and his lack of interest in affairs of state. His enemies in the mountains decided to take advantage of his weakness. Attacks increased on those who strayed from the valley of Tenochtitlán. It appeared that the enemies would soon storm the pass between the two mountains. Tenochtitlán would be blocked off from the rest of the world. They would slaughter the emperor, his daughter, and all the chief warriors. Then the enemies would claim the lands as their own.

The old emperor tried to decide what to do. If he did not act quickly enough, all his people would become slaves of his enemies. His treasured and talented daughter would never become their ruler. After many sleepless nights, he finally realized what he must do. He was filled with bitterness, but he went ahead with his plan.

The next morning he gathered all the best warriors

around him. Those who had distinguished themselves
in battle were there, including Popocatepetl. The
emperor glared at them and spoke as follows:

"Our beautiful kingdom is surrounded by the worst
enemies. We are under attack. In the old days, I would
have risked my life to lead you to victory. Now I am too
old, too weak. My only comfort is that my days are at
an end. Soon, a better ruler than I will take this throne.
Which one of you thinks that he can take my place?
Let him lead our warriors to victory against those who
threaten us. His reward will be my kingdom as well as
my greatest treasure."

As soon as he finished, each warrior shouted that he
should be the one to lead the others to victory. The
emperor silenced them.

"Then go, all of you, and face our enemies. We will
see who is the bravest in battle. When our enemies are
defeated, I shall cease to be emperor. He who has

defeated them will receive the hand of my daughter in marriage. Together, the two of you will rule Tenochtitlán."

When Popocatepetl heard the reward, his heart filled with hope. Without fear, he began preparing to face the enemy. All he could think of was that he had found a way to win the hand of his beloved.

He sharpened the obsidian blade of his hatchet until it was thin enough to slice off a man's head. He made a shield of the thickest animal hide and hardened his cotton armor with brine. He gathered together under his command a group of his most trusted warriors. Then he sent a message to Ixtacihuatl, asking her to meet him secretly by the lake.

The lovers met by the great lake in the middle of the night. When Ixtacihuatl learned of the risks he was about to take, she cried with fear. Yet the idea of his victory filled her with hope. She sent him on to battle with her blessings.

The emperor's words served their purpose. Each of his most talented warriors led his own group of soldiers into battle. These many bands covered the mountainsides around Tenochtitlán. They forced the enemies from their hiding places. The battles were bloody and long. Some of the warriors who dreamed of marrying Ixtacihuatl were killed. Others retreated and joined the troops of those who were braver.

Popocatepetl never gave up. As warriors were killed, his group grew smaller and smaller. Yet he fought fearlessly at their head, despite the increasing danger.

Finally, Popocatepetl was able to drive the last surviving enemies out of the mountains. The enemy fled, as he led his warriors in pursuit. The war against the enemy had been won.

Everyone agreed that Popocatepetl was responsible for crushing the enemy. The men began the homeward journey, eager to tell the emperor of their victory and of Popocatepetl's role in it. However, there were some jealous warriors. They felt that Popocatepetl's triumph was their loss. Eager for power and riches, they hurried ahead of the returning soldiers. They hoped to trick the emperor into thinking that they had won the war.

The warriors who arrived before the others went directly to the emperor. However, the emperor was weak. He could not read the vicious lies on their faces. He was overjoyed that they had triumphed and asked who was responsible for the victory. That man would become ruler and receive the hand of his daughter.

Since the warriors all wanted the reward, they did not know how to answer. Each one was afraid that the others would accuse him of lying if he claimed responsibility for the victory. So the men remained silent. The emperor became suspicious. He asked what had happened to Popocatepetl.

"He is dead," blurted out one of the lying warriors. "He was running from the enemy in great fear. He was chased to the edge of Lake Texcoco and was murdered there. Then his body was tossed into the waters."

The explanation puzzled the emperor. He knew that Popocatepetl was a fearless warrior. He summoned his daughter and told her that the war had been won. Yet his head hung heavy on his chest when he saw the hope shining in her eyes.

"What is the matter, father?" asked Ixtacihuatl.

"My daughter," said the emperor. "Popocatepetl is dead. He was killed near the waters of Texcoco."

Ixtacihuatl turned pale and walked silently from the room. That evening, she climbed the smaller of the two mountains that bordered the pass to her kingdom. She lay down on the mountaintop and asked the earth to take her. As night passed, huge snowflakes fell from the sky. Ixtacihuatl lay still as they covered her. Soon she was buried by snow. The three snowy peaks of a volcano, shaped like a sleeping woman, were all that was left of her. It was as if she had become part of the mountain.

The day after this happened, Popocatepetl returned with his rejoicing warriors. They went to the palace to tell the emperor of their success. They found him near death and broken by grief. After the death of his beloved daughter, he had no more reason to live. However, when he saw Popocatepetl, he exclaimed, "You did not die!" Together, Popocatepetl and his warriors explained the details of their triumph. The old emperor became enraged.

"You and I have been betrayed," he told Popocatepetl. "Those who arrived here first told me that you had been killed and tried to claim your victory as their own."

When he heard about the betrayal, Popocatepetl burned with anger. He vowed to revenge himself upon the lying soldiers, but first he asked where his beloved was. The old emperor buried his face in his hands and mumbled that Ixtacihuatl had died from grief.

Popocatepetl left the palace with a face of stone. He and his warriors hunted those who had lied, one by one. They cut off their heads with sharp hatchets. Then Popocatepetl walked to the top of the larger of the two mountains that overlooked the pass. He lay down and waited patiently for the first snowfall. Soon he was covered with snow and became one with the mountain.

His body became a volcano that from time to time sends up clouds of smoke and fire. The smoke wafts gently into the clear mountain air. It is a tribute to Ixtacihuatl's grace, beauty, and intelligence. Occasionally, the volcano erupts with fiery ashes and boiling lava. These are a sign that Popocatepetl's grief and anger over the loss of his lover last to this day.

READING FOR UNDERSTANDING

1. Describe Popocatepetl's qualities. Why was the emperor wary of him despite these qualities?
2. What qualities did Ixtacihuatl have that would make her a good ruler? Did she want to be the next ruler? Was there anything she wanted more?
3. As the emperor grew weaker and more ill, he focused less on his duties and more on training his daughter. What effect did this have on his enemies? What was their plan?
4. If the emperor thought of his daughter as the next ruler, why did he tell the warriors that whoever would be victorious against the enemies would receive the kingdom as a reward?
5. What happened to Ixtacihuatl and Popocatepetl? Why do you think they were "doomed"?

RESPONDING TO THE STORY

In the tale, envy drove some warriors to spread false rumors that Popocatepetl had died, in order to trick the emperor into thinking they had won the war. Have you ever felt envious over someone else's good fortune? Have you ever tried to take credit for someone else's success, or has someone else tried to take credit for your success? What happened?

REVIEWING VOCABULARY

1. Something that is made of *obsidian* is **(a)** hard and dark **(b)** soft and light **(c)** cold and wet.
2. *Javelins* are used by **(a)** bakers **(b)** judges **(c)** hunters.
3. *Brine* tastes **(a)** sweet **(b)** sour **(c)** salty.
4. A *wary* person is **(a)** tired **(b)** cautious **(c)** sad.
5. If noises *cease*, they **(a)** stop **(b)** increase **(c)** lessen.

6. The cat was in *pursuit* of **(a)** a bowl of milk **(b)** a nap **(c)** a mouse.
7. Being *betrayed* makes you feel **(a)** happy **(b)** angry **(c)** tired.
8. If I *vowed* to do something, then I had **(a)** thought about doing it **(b)** decided to do it **(c)** refused to do it.
9. Which *wafts* through the air? A **(a)** jet **(b)** kite **(c)** tree.
10. A *tribute* shows **(a)** directions **(b)** praise **(c)** disagreement.

THINKING CRITICALLY

1. This tale gave you some insight into Aztec culture. What traits were admired in a ruler? How did the emperor feel about his daughter being a ruler? What traits were admired in a warrior?
2. Describe the emperor's character. What were his beliefs? What were his actions and the consequences of his actions? How might the story have been different if he hadn't opposed the marriage of Ixtacihuatl and Popocatepetl?
3. What other doomed lovers have you read about or seen in the movies? Are their stories similar to the myth you just read? What makes their stories so powerful?

SEÑOR COYOTE AND THE TRICKED TRICKSTER

a Mexican folktale

By I.G. Edmonds

The trickster outwits others and pulls pranks. Well-known trickster characters are the fox in Aesop's fables, Brer Rabbit, and Anansi the spider in African tales.

In Native American stories, one of the great tricksters is the coyote character. Found all over North America, it is quite adaptable. It is quick and sly and will even play dead in order to attract its prey.

It is no wonder, then, that the coyote is often used in stories to represent a character who lives by its wits. Yet, for all its shrewdness, the coyote sometimes meets its match. He certainly does in this story, from Mexico.

VOCABULARY WORDS

spirited (SPIHR-iht-ihd) lively, energetic
❖ The *spirited* horse led all the others around the track.

peon (PEE-ahn) an unskilled worker or farm worker
❖ The *peon* barely made enough money to feed his family.

reproachfully (rih-PROHCH-fuhl-lee) in a way that accuses or blames
❖ "We missed the train again," she said *reproachfully*.

mere (MEER) nothing else than; only
❖ He said he had a *mere* bump and told us not to worry.

indignantly (ihn-DIHG-nuhnt-lee) in a way that shows anger at unjust treatment
❖ The boy said *indignantly* that he didn't break the window.

retorted (rih-TAWR-tihd) answered sharply
❖ When I told her I didn't like that game, she *retorted* that I could leave if I didn't want to play.

budged (BUJD) moved a little bit
❖ The tired children never *budged* from their seats.

welfare (WEHL-fair) state of being or doing well
❖ The neighbors worried about the *welfare* of the sad child.

KEY WORD

caballeros (kab-uh-LEHR-ohs) Spanish for *gentlemen* or *horsemen*
❖ The *caballeros* rode into town on horseback.

One day long ago in Mexico's land of sand and giant cactus Señor Coyote and Señor Mouse had a quarrel.

None now alive can remember why, but recalling what spirited *caballeros* these two were, I suspect that it was some small thing that meant little.

Be that as it may, these two took their quarrels seriously and for a long time would not speak to each other.

Then one day Mouse found Señor Coyote caught in a trap. He howled and twisted and fought, but he could not get out. He had just about given up when he saw Señor Mouse grinning at him.

"Mouse! *Mi viejo amigo*—my old friend!" he cried. "Please gnaw this leather strap in two and get me out of this trap."

"But we are no longer friends," Mouse said. "We have quarreled, remember?"

"Nonsense!" Señor Coyote cried. "Why I love you better than I do Rattlesnake, Owl, or anybody in the desert. You must gnaw me loose. And please hurry for if the peon catches me I will wind up a fur rug on his wife's kitchen floor."

Mouse remembered how mean Señor Coyote had been to him. He was always playing tricks on Mouse and his friends. They were very funny to Coyote for he was a great trickster, but often they hurt little Mouse.

"I'd like to gnaw you free," he said, "but I am old and my teeth tire easily."

"Really, Señor Mouse, you are ungrateful," said Señor Coyote reproachfully. "Remember all the nice things I have done for you."

"What were they?"

"Why—" Coyote began and stopped. He was unable to think of a single thing. There was good reason for this. He had done nothing for Mouse but trick him.

But Señor Coyote is a sly fellow. He said quickly, "Oh, why remind you of them. You remember them all."

"I fear my memory of yesterday is too dim," Mouse said, "but I could remember very well what you could do for me tomorrow."

"Tomorrow?" Coyote asked.

"Yes, tomorrow. If I gnaw away the leather rope holding you in the trap, what will you do for me tomorrow and the day after tomorrow and the day after the day after tomorrow and the day—"

"Stop!" Señor Coyote cried. "How long is this going on?"

"A life is worth a life. If I save your life, you should work for me for a lifetime. That is the only fair thing to do."

"But everyone would laugh at a big, brave, smart fellow like me working as a slave for a mere mouse!" Señor Coyote cried.

"Is that worse than feeling sad for you because your hide is a rug in the peon's kitchen?"

Señor Coyote groaned and cried and argued, but finally agreed when he saw that Mouse would not help him otherwise.

"Very well," he said tearfully, "I agree to work for you until either of us die or until I have a chance to get even by saving your life."

Mouse said with a sly grin, "That is very fine, but I remember what a great trickster you are. So you must also promise that as soon as I free you that you will not jump on me, threaten to kill me, and then save my life by letting me go!"

"Why, how can you suggest such a thing!" Coyote cried indignantly. And then to himself he added, "This mouse is getting *too* smart!"

"Very well, promise," Mouse said.

"But I am not made for work," Señor Coyote said

tearfully. "I live by being sly."

"Then be sly and get out of the trap yourself," Mouse retorted.

"Very well," Señor Coyote said sadly. "I will work for you until I can pay back the debt of my life."

And so Mouse gnawed the leather strap in two and Coyote was saved. Then for many days thereafter Señor Coyote worked for Mouse. Mouse was very proud to have the famous Señor Coyote for a servant. Señor Coyote was greatly embarrassed since he did not like being a servant and disliked working even more.

There was nothing he could do since he had given his promise. He worked all day and dreamed all night of how he could trick his way out of his troubles. He could think of nothing.

Then one day Baby Mouse came running to him. "My father has been caught by Señor Snake!" he cried. "Please come and save him!"

"Hooray!" cried Coyote. "If I save him, I will be released from my promise to work for him."

He went out to the desert rocks and found Señor Rattlesnake with his coils around Señor Mouse.

"Please let him go and I will catch you two more mice," Coyote said.

"My wise old mother used to tell me that a bird in the hand is worth two in the bush," Snake replied. "By the same reasoning, one mouse in Snake's stomach is worth two in Coyote's mind."

"Well, I tried, Mouse," Coyote said. "I'm sorry you must be eaten."

"But you must save me, then you will be free from your promise to me," Mouse said.

"If you're eaten, I'll be free anyway," Señor Coyote said.

"Then everyone will say that Coyote was not smart enough to trick Snake," Mouse said quickly. "And I think they will be right. It makes me very sad for I always thought Señor Coyote the greatest trickster in the world."

This made Coyote's face turn red. He was very proud that everyone thought him so clever. Now he just *had* to save Mouse.

So he said to Snake, "How did you catch Mouse anyway?"

"A rock rolled on top of him and he was trapped," Mouse said. "He asked me to help him roll it off. When I did he jumped on me before I could run away."

"That is not true," Snake said. "How could a little mouse have the strength to roll away a big rock? There is the rock. Now you tell me if you think Mouse could roll it."

It was a very big rock and Coyote admitted that Mouse could not possibly have budged it.

"But it is like the story *Mamacita* tells her children at bedtime," Mouse said quickly. "Once there was a poor burro who had a load of hay just as large as he could carry. His master added just one more straw and the poor burro fell in the dirt. Snake did not have quite enough strength to push the rock off himself. I came along and was like that last straw on the burro's back and together we rolled the rock away."

"Maybe that is true," Snake said, "but by Mouse's own words, he did only a very little of the work. So I owe him only a very little thanks. That is not enough to keep me from eating him."

"Hmmm," said Coyote. "Now you understand, Snake, that I do not care what happens myself. If Mouse is eaten, I will be free of my bargain anyway. I am only thinking of your own welfare, Snake."

"Thank you," said Señor Rattlesnake, "but I do enough thinking about my welfare for both of us. I don't need your thoughts."

"Nevertheless," Coyote insisted, "everyone is going to say that you ate Mouse after he was kind enough to help you."

"I don't care," Snake said. "Nobody says anything good of me anyway."

"Well," said Coyote, "I'll tell you what we should do. We should put everything back as it was. Then I will see for myself if Mouse was as much help as he said he was or as little as you claim. Then I can tell everyone that you were right, Snake."

"Very well," said Señor Snake. "I was lying like this and the rock was on me—"

"Like this?" Coyote said, quickly rolling the rock across Snake's body.

"Ouch!" said Snake. "That is right."

"Can you get out?" Coyote asked.

"No," said Snake.

"Then turn Mouse loose and let him push," said Coyote.

This Snake did, but before Mouse could push, Coyote said, "But on second thought if Mouse pushes, you would then grab him again and we'd be back arguing. Since you are both as you were before the argument started, let us leave it at that and all be friends again!"

Then Coyote turned to Mouse. "So, my friend, I have now saved your life. We are now even and my debt to you is paid."

"But mine is such a *little* life," Mouse protested. "And yours is much *larger.* I don't think they balance. You should still pay me part."

"This is ridiculous!" Coyote cried. "I—"

"Wait!" Snake put in hopefully. "Let me settle the quarrel. Now you roll the rock away. I'll take Mouse in my coils just the way we were when Coyote came up. We'll be then in a position to decide if—"

"Thank you," said Mouse. "It isn't necessary to trouble everyone again. Señor Coyote, we are even."

READING FOR UNDERSTANDING

1. Why did Señor Coyote need Mouse's help?
2. Did Mouse want to help Coyote? What kind of friendship did they have?
3. Explain how Mouse was just as good a trickster as Coyote.
4. What does the expression "A bird in the hand is worth two in the bush" mean? How did Snake explain his behavior with that proverb?
5. There is another proverb that says "Pride goes before a fall." (Pride is an overly high opinion of oneself.) What does this mean? Whom do you think it describes? Explain why.

RESPONDING TO THE STORY

The storyteller says that Coyote thought the jokes he played on Mouse were funny, but they often hurt little Mouse. Did anyone ever play a trick on you that made you want to get even? What did you do?

REVIEWING VOCABULARY

1. A *spirited* discussion is **(a)** spooky **(b)** boring **(c)** lively.
2. A *peon* would most likely **(a)** have a college degree **(b)** work on a farm **(c)** make a large salary.
3. I might look at you *reproachfully* if **(a)** I lost your book **(b)** you lost my book **(c)** you bought me a book.
4. If someone has a *mere* cut, then that person **(a)** is in a lot of pain **(b)** needs a doctor **(c)** should hardly notice it.
5. I might walk out the door *indignantly* if I **(a)** felt insulted **(b)** was late for work **(c)** hurt my foot.
6. If I *retorted* to his question, I **(a)** ignored it **(b)** answered it sharply **(c)** asked him to repeat it.

7. The man never *budged* the whole day. This means he never **(a)** spoke **(b)** moved **(c)** slept.

8. If I am concerned about your *welfare,* then I care about **(a)** how you are **(b)** what you are **(c)** where you are.

THINKING CRITICALLY

1. How do the characters in this story prove the statement "People can be very convincing when there is something to be gained"? Use examples from the story in your response.

2. The title of this story is "Señor Coyote and the Tricked Trickster." Who is the "tricked trickster"? Can it be more than one character? Explain.

3. Mouse said to Coyote, "A life is worth a life. If I save your life, you should work for me for a lifetime. That is the only fair thing to do." Do you agree with Mouse? How do you think a favor or a debt should be repaid?

THE STORY OF THE LAZY MAN WHO GOT TO BE KING OF A TOWN

a Mayan folktale from Guatemala

By Ignacio Bizarro Ujpán
Translated and edited by James D. Sexton

Some people succeed by pure luck. They just happen to be in the right place at the right time. Are these people any less deserving of their success than those who work hard?

Read the following tale about a man who just likes being lazy but who winds up being a king. Could the storyteller be saying something about values, such as loyalty or sincerity, above hard work?

VOCABULARY WORDS

maintenance (MAYN-tuh-nuhns) upkeep; means of support
❖ She never realized all the *maintenance* involved in owning a house.

reverence (REHV-uhr-uhns) feeling of deep respect and love
❖ He looked at his grandfather with *reverence*.

recourse (REE-kawrs) where someone looks for aid or safety
❖ They had no other *recourse* but to stay the night in a shelter.

prophesy (PRAHF-uh-sy) predict
❖ The old magician said he could *prophesy* the future.

nullify (NUL-uh-fy) make useless; cancel
❖ I asked the bank to *nullify* the check.

KEY WORDS

veladoras (vay-lah-DOHR-ahs) Spanish for short, thick candles
❖ He lit three *veladoras* for his brothers.

dueño (DWAY-nyoh) Spanish for master
❖ The *dueño* of the hill had white hair.

lavadero (lah-vah-DEH-roh) Spanish for public wash place
❖ The women walked with their baskets to the *lavadero*.

Earlier, there was a man by the name of Tomás. But mostly they called him Lazy Man because this man didn't want to work. More than anything else, he would pass the time underneath the trees, sleeping.

His father told him, "Tomás, go to work. We need corn and other things for the maintenance of the house."

Tomás answered his father, "I don't want to work. Each time that I work, my stomach hurts. For me, it's better to rest all the time. I like to be lazy."

His father replied, "Tomás, what is this, you don't want to work? We men have the obligation to work, and through work we eat."

The son answered his father, "Papá, I have no desire, nor do I want to work. I prefer to be the best lazy man of the town." And he told him, "Papá, I am lazy, but I know that the lazy men also find their food, and like that, I will do it."

Then the father told him, "Tomás, I have loved you more than your brothers, but from now on, you are on your own, because you dishonor me. Don't you see that in the town they have much respect for me? I even receive reverence."

Tomás told his father, "My good father, from now on you won't have to look at me anymore. I have to leave the house. I already said that I will be the best lazy man."

He grabbed his bundle and went out of the house. Then his father told him, "My son, how dare you abandon the house, but if you think like that, you must leave. There's no other recourse. What I can give you is only a little bit of money to buy your food. When you finish this money, you will remember me, but it is no longer possible to have you in my house."

Tomás took to the road, but with the money that his

father gave him he bought four *veladoras*. Upon arriving at the foot of the hill where one could see his town, he said, "I light the first *veladora* to ask for forgiveness for not respecting my father." After that, he stated, "I light the second *veladora* so that my mother will forgive me. To her I owe my life." And last, he said, "I light the third *veladora* in the name of my town because there I was born, there I grew up, and I don't know if I will see it again."

Tomás, with much laziness, climbed up the slope until he arrived at the summit of the hill. There the night fell upon him and he slept under some trees. At midnight, Tomás got up and lit the last *veladora* for the *dueño* of this hill, saying, "This *veladora* is to ask the *dueño* of this hill for the blessing of my protection. The truth is that in life I don't want to work. Better, in life I want to be Lazy Tomás. I hope that the *dueño* of the hill talks to me in my sleep." He lit the *veladora* and continued sleeping.

Suddenly, a very tall man with white hair came to him and told him, "Tomás, I am the *dueño* of this hill; to me you offer this *veladora*. Well, what do you want me to do for you?"

Tomás, very frightened, answered, "Señor, if you are the *dueño* of this hill, for you is this *veladora* as a present. I want a blessing for my protection in my life. The truth is, I don't want to work, only to be a lazy man."

The *dueño* of the hill told him, "Tomás, you are lazy. Well, I will help you in your life but with the condition that you not forget me. Always light my *veladora* when you find money."

Tomás told him, "Señor of white hairs, tell me, how can I obtain money without work?"

Then the *dueño* of the hill answered him, "When you arrive in the very next town, remain seated close to the *lavadero* in the center of the town. Then the daughter of the king will arrive to wash clothes. You will see well which side she goes to place herself when she washes the clothes. The daughter of the king is tall, slender, and well dressed. She won't realize it when she loses the ring of gold that she is wearing. I will numb her senses. When she finds out about the ring, then she will start to look but won't find it. Then her father, the king, will send to call all the magicians of the town to prophesy where the ring is found. They will not tell the truth. I will nullify the science of the magicians. Then the king will release a public announcement throughout all the town, 'The one who hands over the gold ring will receive a grand prize, half the goods of the kingdom.' But no one will hand it over. Find a long cane and sit in the streets, always like a lazy man. In the dream I will tell you what you will do."

"Thank you, señor. I will do all that you tell me," replied Tomás.

When it dawned, Tomás continued on his way until arriving at the town. There he sat close to the *lavadero* of the town, but on that day, not one woman came to wash. Tomás was all day and all night sleeping there. He thought, maybe the woman will arrive at night to wash, but no.

Dawn came. Tomás sat again to watch. As the sun came out, the daughter of the king arrived to wash clothes. Tomás took good notice where the woman was washing.

The following day, there was a great commotion in the house of the king because his daughter had lost the gold ring. The daughter of the king offered a lot of money to the person who could find the ring, but it was not possible to find it. The king sent to call all the magicians of the town to divine where the ring was to be found, but the magicians could not foresee. Then the king sent a public announcement to all the town to find out who picked up the ring. "The one who returns it will have a reward that is half of the kingdom," but no one could hand over the gold ring.

By the night of that day, Tomás remained sleeping in the hallway of a house, when in his sleep, the señor of white hairs, *dueño* of the hill, spoke to him, telling him, "I am the *dueño* of the hill where you lit a *veladora* as a present. Also, I talked to you on the hill, and I told you that in the dream I will tell you what you will do. Well now, when it dawns, you will be seated at the entrance of the palace of the king, always with the cane in your hand. I will make sure that she talks to you. When she asks you who you are, you will tell her that you are 'Tomás, the wisest.' She will ask you whether with science you can predict the finding of the gold ring that she had lost. You tell her with much assurance that within two days you will tell her where the ring is. She will tell her father. Then when the king receives you in his palace and asks you, 'Who are you?' you will tell him that you are 'Tomás, the wisest.' He will tell you about the ring, and you will tell him with much assurance that within two days you will tell him where the lost object can be found. When the day arrives, tell the king to gather all the people so that you will do these things in their presence. You go ahead with the cane in your hand, and when you reach the *lavadero,* stick the cane inside the pool. Act as if the cane were advising you of something—shake your head. When you arrive in the place where the daughter of the king was washing, there will be the ring, but always have the cane in the water. Stand on that place and tell the king to order a soldier to get into the pool to take out the gold ring. Then hand it over to the woman. In this matter, you will beat all the best magicians of the town, and when they give you your prize, don't forget my *veladora,* always there on the hill where you slept beneath the trees when I talked to you."

Tomás sat down at the entrance of the palace. When the daughter of the king came out, she asked him,

"Hombré, why are you seated here? Who are you?"

And Tomás answered her, "I am Tomás, the wisest of all."

Then the daughter of the king told him, "If you are wise, I want you to tell me the truth. Who has my gold ring that I lost a few days ago?"

Tomás answered her, "Well, I can tell you where the ring is found, but I need two days to not fail."

Then the daughter of the king ran to tell her father that at the entrance of the palace there was a wise man. Then, moved, the king sent a soldier to call Tomás.

In the palace, the king asked him, "Who are you? From where did you come?"

And he answered, "I come from a town. I am the wisest of all."

Then the king told him, "My daughter lost her gold ring. We have looked through all the town, and I sent to call all the magicians of the town, but no one would tell the truth where it was. Now, if you are wise, I want you to tell me where the lost ring is, and I will give you a prize, half of my goods."

Tomás told him, "Señor, if you are the king of this town, with much pleasure, within two days I will tell you with assurance where the ring is found, so get my prize ready."

When the day arrived, Tomás told the king to gather the people of the town so that they would see how a wise man acts. The king did all that Tomás told him. When the town was already gathered, Tomás told them, "Let's go," and he went ahead with the cane in his hand up to where the *lavadero* of the town was located.

The people gathered around and he started to stick the cane inside the *lavadero*, acting as if he were receiving notices from the cane. Tomás, shaking his head, made turns around the *lavadero*. At last, he arrived in the place where the daughter of the king had been washing. There he remained standing with the cane inside the pool, and he told the king, "The ring is here inside the *lavadero*. Your daughter lost the ring when she was washing clothes." Tomás found the ring directly and handed it to the daughter of the king. There then was the fame of Tomás, the wise.

The king told him, "Tomás, you are the wisest one. There is no other wise man like you. Now I give you half of my land, half my young bulls, plus half the money that I have in the treasury. And if I had two women, I would give you one, but I only have one. But, when I die, you stay in my place."

When all that the *dueño* of the hill had told him had been fulfilled, Tomás took more *veladoras*. He went to the hill at midnight, lit the *veladoras,* and soon, the *dueño* of the hill came out and told him, "Thank you for the *veladoras*. I provided all that I promised you. Now you are the best lazy man in the town. The king will die within twenty days, and then you will be king. Then what you want will be fulfilled: you will be like a lazy man because kings don't work. They spend their lives in their palaces."

The king died at the end of twenty days. Then Lazy Tomás remained in place of the king. That is how Lazy Tomás got to be king.

READING FOR UNDERSTANDING

1. Arrange the following incidents in the order in which they occurred:
   (a) Tomás found the ring of the king's daughter
   (b) Tomás went to the king's house.
   (c) Tomás met the *dueño* of the hill.
   (d) Tomás bought four *veladoras*.
   (e) Tomás went to the *lavadero* to watch the king's daughter do the wash.

2. What did Tomás want more than anything?

3. Tomás told his father: "Papa, I am lazy, but I know that the lazy men also find their food, and like that, I will do it." What does this tell you about Tomás?

4. The *dueño* agreed to help Tomás under what condition?

5. What did the lighting of each of the veladoras tell you about Tomás?

6. Do you think Tomás was a good king? Why or why not?

RESPONDING TO THE STORY

Some people think this story was told by someone who valued loyalty above all else. Others say it is about reason versus magic. Still others think it may be making a statement about kings. What do you think? Give details from the story to support your opinion.

REVIEWING VOCABULARY

The following sentences are based on the story. Decide which of the words following the sentences best fits each blank. Write your answers on a separate sheet of paper.

1. Tomás would not help with the _____ of the house.

2. The father received _____ from everyone but Tomás, so he had no other _____ but to tell Tomás to leave.

3. Tomás took the money his father gave him and bought four _____, lighting the last one for the _____ of the hill.

4. This wise man told Tomás to go to the _____ and watch where the king's daughter dropped her ring.

5. He promised that he would _____ the power of the magicians who might _____ where the ring was.

Words: *bless,* dueño, lavadero, *maintenance, nullify, palace, prophesy, recourse, reverence,* veladoras

THINKING CRITICALLY

1. What does this story tell you about some of the religious beliefs of the Mayan people? Give examples from the story.

2. Tomás doesn't tell the king's daughter where the ring is the first time he speaks to her. Explain this in terms of the plot as well as in terms of the art of telling a good story.

3. Tomás doesn't want to work, and this is considered to be a bad character trait by his father. But Tomás has many positive traits also. List at least three, and give an example of each one.

THE BOW, THE DEER, AND THE TALKING BIRD

a Mexican folktale

Retold by Anita Brenner

"Knowledge is power" is a saying that was first written down in Europe in 1597. This story makes clear that, when the Spanish conquered the Aztecs in 1521, Aztecs were well aware of the truth of this saying.

The rich Aztec folktale tradition centers on stories about brave warriors and invading armies. This is not surprising since their large empire was assembled by taking over other empires and smaller nations. But, as you will see, woven into these tales were often lessons about human nature.

In "The Bow, the Deer and the Talking Bird," the youngest son of a dying Aztec merchant must take as his inheritance what his two older brothers do not want. But what they reject is a talking bird whose observations and secrets turn out to be quite important to the young man. The bird provides knowledge.

VOCABULARY WORDS

envy (EHN-vee) dislike for someone who has what you want
* When he saw his neighbor's new car, he was filled with *envy*.

plumes (PLOOMZ) large, showy feathers
* The vase was filled with colorful *plumes*.

gabby (GAB-ee) talkative
* My aunt is so *gabby*, it's hard to get her off the phone.

distressed (dihs-TREHST) filled with sorrow or pain
* They were *distressed* to hear the bad news.

perched (PERCHT) sat
* The bird *perched* on the branch until it saw a worm.

obliged (uh-BLYJD) bound by promise or duty
* He felt *obliged* to carry out his father's last wish.

reputation (rehp-yoo-TAY-shuhn) how one is regarded by others
* Because of the mayor's *reputation*, she easily won the next election.

avenge (uh-VEHNJ) get revenge
* The warriors came to *avenge* the death of their leader.

A rich **Aztec merchant was dying** and he called his three sons and said, "My sons, my time upon this earth is ended. I have tried to be a loyal friend, an honest merchant, and a brave warrior. I have educated you as well as I was able and I hope that if I have any enemies it is more because of their envy than for any wickedness of mine. Besides my advice and example, I wish to leave you three things. If managed properly, they will be better than the greatest riches. These three things are a bow that always sends the arrow true to its aim, a deer that will take his master anywhere he wants to go, and a bird that speaks of what it sees." He died.

The eldest son said, "As I am the eldest, I should have first choice of the inheritance. I choose the bow." For he thought to himself, "With a bow like that I can kill the rarest birds and become a rich trader in fine feathers and plumes."

The second son said, "Between a gabby-bird and a deer that will take me anywhere I want to go, I choose the deer."

So the youngest son took what was left; the bird. He thought, "I will take care of it lovingly, there may not be much use in a bird like that but it belonged to my dear father." Then they all went off to seek their fortunes.

Many years later the two oldest brothers heard that the youngest one was now a great and famous man. He was the Prime Minister to the king. His advice and warnings and opinions were listened to, for they were always wise and true. The two brothers became very jealous when they heard this, and they plotted to kill him, steal the bird that they had so thoughtlessly refused, and take their brother's place. They well knew that it was the wonderful bird that had made him Prime Minister.

They did not notice that while they were talking, the

very same bird was sitting on a branch above their heads. He heard them, and flew to tell the youngest son. Tears came to his eyes. "Alas," he said, "I am not afraid of my brothers. I can take care of myself, but my poor father's ghost must be distressed to learn that his sons are unworthy of him. I do not think they are really bad at heart. Let us see what can be done."

The next day the two brothers arrived at the king's court. They pretended to be overcome with surprise and joy at their youngest brother's luck in being such an important man. He received them with tears in his eyes and gave them the best rooms in the palace, and introduced them to the king, too. The brothers went to sleep early, for the eldest was tired from walking so far and the second brother had a sore throat from the dust that his deer had made as it ran swiftly along the roads.

The youngest son sat down as he did every evening to listen to his little bird. The bird perched on his shoulder and said softly, "The king of the country next to ours has decided to make war on us and conquer us. He wants to take us by surprise. His army will march against us and attack early tomorrow morning. They will take the road that lies below the steep cliff at the mouth of the river." When the bird finished whispering this information into his master's ear, he flew away. But the young man went to the king at once and told him what was going to happen.

"Oh dear, oh dear," said the king. "Our best captains are off on a picnic and the soldiers are having a holiday. What shall we do?"

"Most worthy Sire," said the youngest brother, "if Your Majesty promises to make nobles of my brothers and myself, we three will save you no matter how strong the enemy turns out to be."

"I promise," said the king, but he didn't have much hope. He didn't see how three young men, no matter how brave, could stop all the armies of his powerful neighbor.

The youngest one hurried to his brothers and woke them. "My brothers," he said, "our father was such a brave man that still today, people say when they hear our name, oh, yes, they are the sons of that warrior who never knew what it was to be afraid. Don't you think we are obliged to uphold his reputation and for the honor of our name, go out and defend our native land?" Then he explained what was going to happen. And he made plans.

"Your little deer," said he to the middle brother, "will take us to the cliff quickly, in plenty of time, because what army can travel as fast and far as a deer? Then when we get there my bird will tell us exactly where the enemy is hiding. And you with your bow," he said to the eldest brother, "can do the shooting."

The three brothers climbed on the deer's back, and the bird perched on the youngest one's shoulder. The middle brother said, "Quickly, quickly, little deer," and in less than a minute, even less than a second, they were at the cliff. They hid in some bushes and the bird went off on a scouting trip, to see what he could see. He came back quickly and told them where the enemy was hidden, and exactly where the king of the attacking soldiers was.

The eldest brother fitted an arrow to his bow, aimed where the little bird told him, and shot. The arrow traveled far away where the wicked king was hiding, whang! through his heart. The army was frightened and bewildered. The soldiers said, "This is very strange, let us go home." But one captain, bolder than the others, jumped up and shouted, "Forward, my brave boys, let us avenge the death of our great and noble king!" The eldest brother fitted another arrow to his bow, aimed at the captain, and the arrow traveled far and fast, whang! And the captain fell dead.

The soldiers began to run back to their own country

as fast as they could. By the time the sun rose they were all gone, running, some on galloping horses, some on foot. The three brothers put the dead king and the dead captain on the deer's back, and they all went home to breakfast.

The people came out to meet them, singing and dancing and cheering. The king made nobles of the three brothers and gave them rich presents, lands, houses, horses, wonderful things. They lived happily after that because they had found out something important: that together they could do more than separately, and that there is nothing better than a good brother. Ever since then, when people know a secret, they say, "Oh, a little bird told me."

READING FOR UNDERSTANDING

1. What were the special qualities of the bow, the deer, and the bird?

2. What did the two older brothers find out about the youngest brother? How did they react?

3. When the older brothers came to the king's court, why did the youngest brother have tears in his eyes as he gave them the best rooms in the palace?

4. Why did the youngest son, who knew about his brothers' greed, make an agreement with the king?

5. Why do you think the two older brothers went along with the youngest brother's plan to save the king?

6. What is the lesson to be learned from this tale? Does it hold true for us today?

RESPONDING TO THE FOLKTALE

Why do you think the youngest brother was so different from his two older brothers? Was it the influence of the bird? If so, explain this influence. If not, give another reason.

REVIEWING VOCABULARY

1. Someone who is filled with *envy* **(a)** just ate a big meal **(b)** is laughing **(c)** wants what someone else has.

2. You would find *plumes* on a **(a)** bird **(b)** cat **(c)** tree.

3. A *gabby* person **(a)** sings **(b)** cries **(c)** talks.

4. You would probably be *distressed* if you **(a)** lost your job **(b)** found a job **(c)** heard about a better job.

5. If the cat was *perched*, it was **(a)** eating **(b)** sitting **(c)** running.

6. If you feel *obliged* to do something, you **(a)** don't want to do it **(b)** feel you have to do it **(c)** aren't sure.

7. Someone's *reputation* is how he or she **(a)** is regarded **(b)** lives **(c)** travels.
8. The man wanted to *avenge* his brother's death by **(a)** crying **(b)** praying **(c)** getting revenge.

THINKING CRITICALLY

1. What did the dying Aztec merchant mean when he told his sons that he had left them an inheritance "better than the greatest riches"?
2. Why do you think each brother chose the item he did? What does each brother's choice tell you about his character?
3. How did the relationship of the brothers change, and what do they learn by the end of the story?
4. The knowledge provided by the bird gave the youngest son an advantage over everyone in the story. List three ways he used this advantage. Do you think he used his power responsibly? Why or why not?

LORD SUN'S BRIDE
a Mayan Tale
Edited by John Bierhorst

Have you ever looked up into the sky at night and seen a full moon shining in three-dimensional clarity? Such a night brings thoughts of the mystery of creation and our dependence on the sun. People have been doing this since the beginning of recorded time. The ancient Egyptians worshipped the moon and the sun.

The Maya of southern Mexico and Central America not only marveled at the moon and sun, but they also observed them scientifically. They developed a calendar based on the movement of the sun.

"Lord Sun's Bride" is a Mayan myth. Like all peoples, the Maya told myths to understand how the world came to be. When the sun seeks a bride, the Maya explain how the moon comes into being. As you read, notice how many other things in nature make their first appearance.

VOCABULARY WORDS

game (GAYM) wild animals that are hunted
❖ The men only hunt where there is plenty of *game*.

exchange (ehks-CHAYNJ) trade; substitution
❖ We baked them a pie in *exchange* for the apples.

nectar (NEHK-tuhr) sweet liquid of a plant
❖ Bees make honey from the *nectar* of flowers.

darting (DAHR-tihng) moving rapidly
❖ She saw the cat *darting* across the street.

loom (LOOM) frame for making yarn into cloth
❖ We no longer have to make cloth with a *loom*.

reviving (rih-VYV-ihng) bringing back to life
❖ The doctor tried *reviving* the man after the accident.

innermost (IH-nuhr-mohst) deepest within
❖ He never knew her *innermost* thoughts.

KEY WORDS

matchmaker (MACH-may-kuhr) one who brings two
people together
❖ The desperate man asked a *matchmaker* to find a
wife for his son.

blowgun (BLOH-guhn) tube that you breathe into to
shoot out a dart
❖ In the jungle, some people hunt with a *blowgun*.

chilies (CHIH-leez) hot peppers, first used by Native
Americans of Central America
❖ The chef uses lots of *chilies* in her dishes.

In a house deep in the woods an old man was living with his only daughter, a pretty young woman who could spin cotton quickly and weave to perfection. Spying on her, the sun decided to make her his wife and thought he would win her on his own, without the help of a matchmaker.

The next day he went hunting, shot a deer, and carried it past the young woman's house. Game was scarce, but Lord Sun had a plan to trick the girl into thinking he was a hunter who always came back with plenty.

Having stuffed the deerskin with ashes and grass and dried leaves, he would take it into the woods every evening after dark and leave it there. Then he would go back to his hut. Early in the morning he would pass by the girl's house empty-handed, returning a little later with the stuffed animal on his shoulder.

"Look, Father," said the old man's daughter, "that hunter shoots game every day. I think he should be my husband."

"Ah," said the old man, "he may be tricking you."

"Oh, no," she replied, "he has to be the one who kills the game. Look at the blood on him."

"Well," said the father, "throw some water on the path when he comes by again, and see what happens."

The girl didn't believe him. But the next time she saw Lord Sun on his way home from hunting, she took some of the lime water she had been using to soak corn and threw it on the path.

Lord Sun slipped and fell. The deerskin burst, and all the ashes and grass and leaves poured out on the ground. The young woman began to laugh, and Lord Sun ran off.

He was ashamed. Then he went to the hummingbird and asked to borrow the bird's skin. The hummingbird at first refused, saying he would die of the cold, agreeing only after Lord Sun had promised to wrap him in cotton. When the exchange had been made, Lord Sun put on the skin, turned into a hummingbird, and flew back to the young woman's house.

From the ashes and leaves that had poured out of the deer hide, a tobacco plant had sprung up, and it was already in flower. Sun flew directly to it and began sucking the nectar, darting from blossom to blossom. When the young woman saw him, she called to her father.

"Look, Father, a hummingbird! Get your blowgun and shoot him. I want him for a pet."

"Very well," said the old man, and he aimed the blowgun so that the bird was only stunned. "Look for it in the grass," he said. When she found it, it was softly chirping: *sweet sweet sweet*. As she stooped down to pick it up, the strap that passed around her waist to hold the loom tight slipped, and the loom fell to the ground.

She carried the hummingbird indoors and, giving it chocolate and corn syrup, succeeded in reviving it. Then she took it to her bedroom, which was the innermost of thirteen rooms, and as the darkness was now coming fast, she laid the bird aside and went to sleep.

In the middle of the night she awoke and found a man lying next to her. It was Lord Sun. "My father will kill me," she said.

"Not if we run away," he replied.

The girl wanted to go with him very much, but she was afraid. Her father, they say, had a magic stone in which he could see everything that was happening in the world. "Give me the stone," said Lord Sun, and when she had brought it to him, he smeared it with soot and told her to put it back in its place. Now, he thought, they could leave without danger of being seen.

But the girl was still afraid, because her father had a magic blowgun with which he could suck anything to him, no matter how far away it might be. "Where is the blowgun?" asked Lord Sun.

"Here," she replied. Then he told her to grind some dried chilies. When the chili pepper was ready, he poured it into the blowgun and told the girl to put it back in its place. As soon as she had done so, they slipped away.

Next morning when the old man awoke, he saw no sign of his daughter and heard no sound in the house. He called to her and got no reply. He looked for her and failed to find her. Then he reached for his magic stone to discover where she might have gone. But he could see nothing because the stone was blackened with soot. At last, however, he found a small spot that Lord Sun had neglected to cover up, and looking closely, he saw his daughter and a young man out on the water in a canoe.

Reaching quickly for his magic blowgun, he put it to his lips and sucked in as hard as he could. The next moment he lay on his back, gasping for air and coughing violently: *ochó, ochó, ochó*. And that was the first coughing in the world.

The old man was furious. "Now they shall die," he said. Then he called to the rain god, Chac, and when Chac arrived, he ordered him to send a thunderbolt to kill the fleeing couple.

Chac protested. "No, I won't kill them. You hate them now and want them dead. But later, when your anger passes, you will be sorry, and you will be angry with me for having killed them."

But the old man insisted. Finally Chac threw on his black clothes, took up his drum and his ax, and departed. Traveling high in the sky, he looked down and caught sight of the canoe.

Sun saw him coming. "Your father has sent Chac to kill us," he cried. "Quick, jump into the water!" Immediately he changed himself into a turtle, and the young woman became a crab, both of them swimming downward as fast as they could.

Lord Sun was far below the surface in no time. But the crab swims slowly, and when the lightning struck, the girl was only a little way down. She was killed instantly, and her blood flowed in all directions.

When the danger had passed, Lord Sun rose to the surface again and saw the young woman's blood in the water. Grief-stricken, he called to the small fish that lived there and asked them to help him. But instead, they began drinking the blood. Then he called to the dragonfly. It answered him: *srrr srrr srrr*. He ordered it to collect all the blood, and it obeyed him at once, filling thirteen water jars. These Lord Sun left in the house of an old woman who lived by the shore, promising to return in thirteen days.

When the thirteen days had passed, he came back and asked for the jars. "Take them away," cried the old woman. "I can't sleep for the noise that comes from inside them, a buzzing and a humming and a rustling."

Lord Sun began to pour out the jars. The first contained nothing but snakes, all kinds of poisonous snakes. The second and third jars were also full of snakes, though not poisonous. The fourth was full of mosquitoes. In the fifth were sand flies; in the sixth, green hornets; in the seventh, yellow wasps; in the eighth, small black wasps; in the ninth, black wasps with white wings; in the tenth, stinging caterpillars; and in the eleventh and twelfth, all sorts of flies. Before this time, these creatures had not been known in the world.

But in the thirteenth jar he found his love, alive again and as beautiful as she had been before. Then he called to a deer and ordered it to carry her into the sky. It did so, and there she remained, becoming our heavenly mother, the moon.

READING FOR UNDERSTANDING

The following paragraphs describe events in the myth. Decide which of the words below the paragraph best fits in each blank. Write your answers on a separate sheet of paper.

Lord Sun's decision to marry resulted in magical changes. When the ashes and leaves fell out of Lord Sun's stuffed **(1)**_____, a **(2)**_____ plant sprang up. Lord Sun dressed in a **(3)**_____ skin and sipped nectar from the blossoms. The woman's father sucked ground **(4)**_____ from his blowgun, placed there by Lord Sun. The father's **(5)**_____ were the first in the world. To escape Chac, the **(6)**_____ god, and his thunderbolts, Lord Sun turned himself into a **(7)**_____ and the young woman into a **(8)**_____. Lord Sun survived the thunderbolts, but the girl was killed, and her **(9)**_____ flowed in all directions. Lord Sun ordered a **(10)**_____ to collect it in **(11)**_____ water jars. From these jars came creatures never seen before, including poisonous **(12)**_____ stinging **(13)**_____, and various kinds of **(14)**_____ and **(15)**_____. Lord Sun found the young woman alive in the last jar and carried her to the sky to become the **(16)**_____.

Words: *wasps, hummingbird, dragonfly, blood, moon, rain, coughs, flies, turtle, deerskin, chilies, snakes, wasps, tobacco, crab, thirteen, caterpillars.*

RESPONDING TO THE MYTH

Select one scene or series of events in the story that made an impression on you. Explain your choice, using details from the myth to support your response.

REVIEWING VOCABULARY

Match each word on the left with the correct definition on the right.

1. loom

a. bringing back to life

2. exchange

b. moving rapidly

3. darting

c. frame for making yarn into cloth

4. reviving

5. innermost

d. deepest within

6. nectar

e. sweet liquid of a plant

7. game

f. trade; substitution

g. wild animals that are hunted

THINKING CRITICALLY

1. Many transformations occured in this story. Describe them, and explain the part they played in the creation myths.

2. The old man was very angry at his daughter and Lord Sun after they tricked him. He even said, "Now they shall die!" and ordered Chac to kill them. Why do you think he tried to kill his own daughter? Do you feel that he was justified? How else might he have handled the situation?

3. The Maya called the sun "Lord Sun" and made the sun a main character in this myth. Why do you think it was so important in their culture? Why did they turn the girl into the moon?

Unit 4

STORIES FROM SOUTH AMERICA

THE BAKER'S NEIGHBOR
a story from Peru
Adapted from a translation by Frank Henius

Do you consider yourself to be a hard-working person? Are you willing to give up things in life in order to reach your goals? Not all people approach life and work in this way.

Some people enjoy life's experiences on a day-to-day basis. They believe the future will bring what it will bring. There is room for both points of view, but conflicts can arise.

In this tale from Peru, a baker and his neighbor find themselves at such odds that they create an uproar in their city. Their dispute can only be solved by a wise judge. Behind the humor in the story is a timeless lesson about human interactions. What questions about values does the story raise?

VOCABULARY WORDS

wares (WAIRZ) articles for sale
❖ He put his *wares* on the table and waited for customers to appear.

profited (PRAHF-ih-tihd) made money; benefited
❖ At the end of the day, he said he *profited* from all the sales.

guffaws (gu-FAWZ) loud bursts of laughter
❖ We could hear their *guffaws* from across the street.

enraged (ehn-RAYJD) very angry
❖ She was *enraged* when I lost her favorite ring.

humiliated (hyoo-MIHL-ee-ay-tihd) made to feel a loss of pride or self-worth
❖ I was *humiliated* when my boss said my report was terrible.

gloated (GLOH-tihd) looked at with selfish satisfaction
❖ She *gloated* over her new car.

plaintiff (PLAYN-tihf) person who brings a complaint in court
❖ The *plaintiff* was suing the man who crashed his truck into her car.

defendant (dih-FEHN-duhnt) person who is accused in court
❖ The *defendant* said that he was innocent.

hoisted (HOIS-tihd) raised up high
❖ The mover *hoisted* the box onto his shoulder.

Once upon a time, more than one hundred years ago, there lived a baker in the city of Lima, in Peru. He was a hardworking man. At night, he mixed flour and kneaded dough and baked his bread and pastries. Early every morning, he opened his shop. All day he sold his wares to the townsfolk and made a lot of money. He loved money better than anything else in the world!

His next-door neighbor was quite a different kind of man. He did not like to work too much and would rather sit in the sun or listen to the birds. He did not care much for money, unlike the bread-and-pastry cook. The neighbor enjoyed life and all the small joys it offered. He took great pleasure in the splendid smell of the freshly baked rolls and cakes, which the morning breeze always brought to his door.

After each night's work, the baker would sit at a table outside his house. He would pull out his purse and, just as the sun rose in the sky, count the money he had taken in. He would inspect each coin. Then for more than an hour he would figure and fret and add and subtract.

His jolly neighbor would get up the moment he heard the baker come into his yard to count coins. The neighbor would go downstairs, lean against the door of the bakery, and inhale the fragrant odors of the freshly baked bread and rolls and cakes. He greatly enjoyed their smell and treasured this free and daily luxury. At the same time, his eyes would rest gratefully on the first golden rays of the bright Peruvian sun.

The baker knew full well that his neighbor seldom bought anything in the shop. Yet he profited every morning by the breeze from the sea that brought the bakery's odors. Whenever he looked up from the money piled on the table, he saw his neighbor taking pleasure from the smell of his breads and pastries. He never said a word, but he was filled with rage at the joy on his neighbor's face. He was also quite angry when he thought how the costly blend of his flour, sugar, raisins, and other ingredients was all enjoyed for free, while he, the baker, had to work most of the night to provide it.

One fine day, the baker decided that he had stood it long enough. He could no longer silently watch as he was deprived of the fruits of his labor and the cost of his supplies without any payment. Going to the neighbor's house, he demanded a large sum of money for the splendid odors he had daily supplied him with for many years without ever sending a bill or collecting any money for them.

The jolly fellow at first did not seem to understand the baker. When he at last realized what it all meant, he laughed right in the angry baker's face. He laughed so loud and so long that all the other neighbors came to ask what made him laugh so much. He told them his story, interrupted by his own and the others' loud guffaws. The baker, enraged and humiliated, returned to his shop.

Soon the whole town of Lima knew of the baker's bill for his pastry smells. Of course, this annoyed the baker still more. He was not only disappointed that he had received no money from his neighbor. He was also angry that he had to stand all the jokes and teasing. Whenever he came out of his shop to go on an errand, the little boys and girls would run after him. They would pretend to sniff at his clothes and his hands. Then they would run in front of him, asking him how much he wanted for the lovely smell they had just enjoyed.

The baker could no longer stand it. He tried once more to get payment from his neighbor so as to close the matter gracefully and stop his humiliation. When he failed and was laughed at and teased more than ever, he decided to fight for the money he felt he was owed. So he took his case to court.

The judge, like most of Lima's citizens, already had heard of the baker and his complaint. As the laws of Peru demanded, he invited the baker to come to court and tell his story. The judge, who had a great sense of humor, listened gravely and told the baker that he would decide the case soon.

The following week, the judge ordered both the baker and the neighbor to appear in court. He ordered the neighbor to bring a bag with one hundred gold coins.

The news of the action and of the judge's order soon spread through the town of Lima. The neighbor began to lose his carefree spirit and behavior. He shook with the fear that he would have to pay for the pastry and bread smells he had been enjoying in the past.

On the other hand, the baker already began to rub his hands and count the gold coins in his mind. He went around happy and grinning. He gloated over the coins as if they were already jingling in his pocket.

A week later, both were in court. All the neighbors and many other citizens of Lima were there, too. They all felt sorry for the jolly fellow who looked so sad. The courtroom hummed from all the noise and talk and whispering. However, when the clerk of the court announced the entry of the judge, they all became silent and rose.

The judge ordered them to be seated. He had the plaintiff, the baker, and defendant, the neighbor, swear that they would tell the truth and nothing but the truth. Then the baker was told to repeat his complaint.

The baker felt he must convince the judge that the odors from his oven were worth at least a hundred gold coins. He spoke for quite a while. He told all about his work. One by one he described the flour, milk, raisins, almonds, and all the other good things that went into his breads and pastries. He then figured their costs in detail. He explained how the odors the neighbor inhaled were the result of all his work and expense. The judge listened gravely.

When the baker finished his story, the judge gave the defendant a hard look. He asked if the morning breeze wafted these costly odors daily to his house. This was admitted by the defendant, who was by now quite downhearted. Then the judge wanted to know if the bread, rolls, and pastry had a pleasing or an annoying smell.

The neighbor, of course, had to admit that the smells were very pleasing. As soon as he had said this, he regretted it. The judge now asked him to hand the bag with the hundred gold coins to the baker.

The baker nearly shouted with joy. He could not keep his arms from shooting out from his body with hands outstretched. He almost fell over the witness-stand railing, so eager was he to grab the bag and get hold of the money.

At last he clutched the bag and pressed it to his chest. He turned to leave and go home with the precious gold. However, the judge then ordered him to step to a big table in front of the bench. There he was told to empty the bag and to count the hundred coins, one by one.

The baker thought this was very kind of the judge. It let him check that he had not been cheated by that good-for-nothing neighbor. At last, the man who had smelled his bakery's odors for years was going to pay for them. So the baker emptied the bag on the large table and began to count.

The gold coins glistened in the sunshine. They jumped and gave a fine, high, metallic sound as they hit the wood. Everyone could see that the shine and sound of the coins were a feast for the eyes and music for the ears of the baker.

The judge, the neighbor, and all the other neighbors and citizens of Lima could also see with what pleasure the baker touched each gold coin. In fact, he could hardly drop one coin to pick up the next. There was no doubt that he enjoyed the touch of the gold, its glint, charm, and sound, as he counted and dropped the coins one by one onto the table.

He lovingly put the coins back into the bag. Then he told the judge that there were indeed one hundred coins and that none of them was false. Before leaving the court, he also wanted to thank the judge for his fair and wise decision. To his surprise and alarm, the judge asked him to hand the bag back to the defendant.

The judge rose from his chair and put on his black cap with the red ribbon. He asked all those in court to stand up. They all rose and stood silently waiting for the decision. In the name of the people of Peru, the judge solemnly gave his judgment:

"The court has heard the baker's complaint against the neighbor and the neighbor's admission that he did enjoy the odors brought to his door. I therefore declare that the case is now settled, Baker. Your neighbor has *smelled* your pastry and bread and you have *seen* and *touched* his gold."

At first, no one fully realized the meaning of this wise judgment. When they did, the hush in the court was suddenly broken. Everyone laughed, cried, shouted, and congratulated the neighbor on his victory.

The neighbor still stood at the rail, puzzled at first. He held the bag with one hand and felt it with the other to make sure that his savings had been returned to him. Then he began to laugh loud and long. Soon the whole court was laughing, except for the baker. He had slipped out of the court, for he realized quicker than anyone else that he had lost his case.

The clerk of the court hammered his gavel, asked the people to be silent, and leave the court. Then they all stood and laughed and shouted in front of the court-house. They hoisted the neighbor on their shoulders.

Joyously noisy, they carried him, gold and all, back to his house.

When the baker saw the group enter his street, he hid behind his curtains. He was ashamed. He also could no longer stand the sight of his neighbor at sunrise, enjoying the bakery smells more than ever. He never went out into the morning light himself. He brought the table and the chair from the yard into his house and counted his money inside.

From that time, many of the neighbors and their friends came to the jolly fellow's house every morning. They laughed and gossiped and some of them even sang. They looked at the sun's golden rays. At the same time they enjoyed the smells of the pastry and bread, wafted to them by the breeze.

Their laughter and gaiety went straight through the door and window to the baker's ears. He sat in a dark corner and counted his money by candlelight. All the while, the jolly neighbor enjoyed the morning breeze and its aroma more than ever before.

READING FOR UNDERSTANDING

The following paragraph summarizes the story. Decide which of the words below the paragraph best fits in each blank. Some words are not used and others are used more than once. Write on a separate paper.

Once there was a **(1)**_____ who loved **(2)**_____ more than anything else in the world. His **(3)**_____ did not care much for **(4)**_____ He enjoyed simple things like smelling the **(5)**_____ of the freshly baked wares. When the **(6)**_____ counted his **(7)**_____, he became angry that the **(8)**_____ enjoyed the smells for free. After the baker gave him a **(9)**_____ for the smells, everyone in the **(10)**_____ made fun of him. When the **(11)**_____ brought his case to **(12)**_____, the **(13)**_____ listened and ordered the **(14)**_____ to bring in a sack of coins. But after the **(15)**_____ had enjoyed **(16)**_____, seeing, and hearing the coins, just as his neighbor had enjoyed smelling the freshly baked wares, the **(17)**_____ told him to give the coins back to his **(18)**_____.

Words: *baker, bill, children, court, flour, judge, money, neighbor, odors, rays, shop, touching, town*

RESPONDING TO THE STORY

The baker's neighbor enjoyed the simple pleasures in life—the sun's golden rays, the chirping of birds, and the aroma of fresh bread. What are the simple pleasures in life that you enjoy or that you would like to enjoy? Write about them, using descriptive language.

REVIEWING VOCABULARY

Match each word on the left with the correct definition on the right.

1. wares

2. profited

3. guffaws

4. enraged

5. humiliated

6. gloated

7. plaintiff

8. defendant

9. hoisted

a. looked at with selfish satisfaction

b. loud bursts of laughter

c. raised up high

d. articles for sale

e. person who is accused in court

f. very angry

g. made money; benefited

h. person who brings a complaint in court

i. made to feel a loss of pride or self-worth

THINKING CRITICALLY

1. In the Greek myth of King Midas, everything that the greedy king touched turned to gold. Midas learned his lesson only after his touch turned his daughter into gold. In this story, the baker's love of gold finally worked against him, too. Do you think the baker learned his lesson from the judge's ruling? Describe his behavior after the ruling. What was missing in the baker's life?

2. The neighbor's behavior changed when the judge ordered him to bring a sack with one hundred coins to court. Describe what happened to him. Why do you think the judge didn't tell him in advance of his plan?

3. What lesson does this story teach? How do we decide which is more valuable—hard work and making money, or enjoying a free and easy life? Is there a middle ground? Explain.

THE GREEN MOSS PRINCE
a story from Uruguay
Translated by Frank Henius

Love is such a powerful emotion. It can bring the greatest joy or the deepest despair. In the name of love, poems have been written, statues carved, tombs built, wars fought. Stories throughout time have told of people who have lived for love and died for love.

In the following tale, as in so many folktales told throughout the world, love is put to the test. In Uruguay, the small country at the southern tip of Brazil, the beautiful and virtuous Florinda is betrayed by untrue friends. Her sweetheart is injured, and he blames Florinda, though she is innocent. He disappears and angrily vows that she will never see him again unless she can accomplish a seemingly impossible task. Once again, we see a character in a folktale who must prove herself to win somebody. She begins her journey to find him. Will she be able to find her way to the Green Moss Prince, and to his heart?

VOCABULARY WORDS

virtuous (VER-choo-uhs) highly moral; very good
❖ The *virtuous* man could be trusted in all things.

dullard (DUL-uhrd) stupid person
❖ She called him a *dullard* because he couldn't fix the car.

entrusted (ehn-TRUS-tihd) given a duty
❖ We were *entrusted* with taking care of their dog.

swarthy (SWAWR-thee) having a dark complexion
❖ The handsome man was tall and *swarthy*.

reproachful (rih-PROHCH-fuhl) full of blame
❖ The judge's attitude to the criminal was *reproachful*.

gaunt (GAWNT) thin and bony
❖ The *gaunt* old woman looked as if she needed a meal.

abode (uh-BOHD) home; residence
❖ That old house was once the *abode* of a famous actor.

whimsical (WHIHM-zih-kuhl) unpredictable
❖ She was *whimsical,* and we couldn't tell what she might say.

entreaties (ehn-TREE-teez) strong requests
❖ He paid no attention to their *entreaties* for money.

plight (PLYT) serious situation
❖ Tears rolled down her cheeks as she told us of her *plight*.

adjoining (uh-JOIN-ihng) side by side
❖ We asked for *adjoining* rooms at the hotel.

esteemed (uh-STEEMD) thought of with high regard
❖ The people in town *esteemed* the soldiers who went to war.

**O**nce upon a time there lived a young girl named Florinda, all by herself, in a small town. Her parents were dead, so, being poor, she had to work very hard to support herself. She was virtuous and beautiful.

There lived in the same town a widow who had three daughters, who had made friends with the attractive orphan girl.

One day while staying in Florinda's home, one of these young ladies discovered, in a corner of the room, some fine and costly jewels, which fact she duly reported to her mother.

"Jewels?" said the latter. "Where do they come from? Why, I always had my doubts about that girl's character, with her pretty manners and ladylike airs."

And calling in her eldest daughter, she said:

*"Juanita, you are going to Florinda's to
spend the night with her, aren't you? Now,
keep your eyes open to see what is going on
there."*

So, welcomed by the unsuspecting Florinda, the girl visited her.

When night came and it was time to retire, the youthful hostess said: "Let us have some tea before going to our beds."

So, laughing and joking, the girls sipped the delicious beverage, undressed, and cozily tucked themselves in bed. It was not long before the widow's daughter was sleeping deeply. When she finally blinked her short-sighted eyes, it was broad daylight.

"You big dullard," her mother remarked, when the girl, after going back home, admitted her failure.

The following night the second daughter was entrusted with a similar mission. The scene of the

previous night repeated itself, and the visitor again
enjoyed a restful sleep, unhaunted by dreams.

The mother was very much enraged by the failure of
the two girls. She was in a very bad humor. Suddenly
her youngest daughter entered the room and begged to
be given the opportunity to discover Florinda's secret.

"Do you believe that, one-eyed as you are, you
would not fail like your two older sisters?"

However, the mother was finally persuaded to let the
girl go and try her luck.

When night came, Florinda said, as on the previous
nights: "Let us treat ourselves to some tea and go to bed."

When, however, she was presented with a cup of tea,
the one-eyed girl, instead of drinking it, poured it onto
her dress. Soon both girls went to bed.

The widow's daughter, her one eye closed, her
swarthy, ugly face buried in the pillow, seemed to be
fast asleep. Cautiously, Florinda crept out of bed and
dressed again. She walked to the mirror and carefully
combed her hair. The one-eyed girl saw it all. Close to
midnight, a flapping of wings was heard outside the
window, followed by repeated beats on the glass pane.
Florinda opened it. Into the bedroom flew a parrot. It
was a large, emerald-green bird. Gently fluttering its
wings, it headed toward a basin filled with water, placed
on the floor of the room. There it plunged, and after
splashing in the water, to the girl's amazement, the parrot was transformed into a young man, all clad in green
velvet, and of a noble and commanding presence.

After kissing his sweetheart, he presented her with a
diamond necklace. The lovers spent several hours
together, but in the hush of morning that precedes
dawn, the prince—for he was a prince—said to
Florinda:

"Now, I have to go. Good-bye, sweetheart."

Stepping into the basin, the green-clad prince

became once more a parrot and flew away.

The following morning, upon hearing the news, the widow gave instructions to her one-eyed daughter.

"While Florinda is away during the day you are going to place pieces of broken glass all around the window, and this razor well in the middle."

The one-eyed girl obeyed.

When, at midnight, the flapping of wings announced the arrival of the bird, instead of the usual beats there was a moment of silence, followed by a reproachful human voice:

> *"You, ungrateful Florinda! So you would kill me! Well, good-bye . . . good-bye forever! You will not see me any more, unless, after having worn out three pairs of iron shoes, you come to my Kingdom of the Green Moss."*

And that was all. Tired, the parrot disappeared in the darkness of the night. The window was splashed with his blood.

Florinda did not let her grief get the better of her. After ordering three pairs of iron shoes, that hurt her tiny, delicate feet, she set out on her journey to the Kingdom of the Green Moss. She walked and walked. Nobody could tell her, however, what road to follow; nobody had ever heard of it. But she kept on. She had already been on the way a whole year, and the first pair of iron shoes was worn out, when one day she saw a house. She knocked on the door.

"Would you let me stay here for the night?" she asked a gaunt, somber woman who had answered her call. "I do not have any place to go."

The old woman's face fell.

"Do you not know that this is my son's, the Wind's abode? When night comes, he rushes home in a fury, uprooting trees and tearing down houses. He would kill you."

"I am as good as dead," answered the poor girl. "Perhaps you know where I can find the Kingdom of the Green Moss?"

"I certainly do not," answered the woman. "My son might know, for he goes everywhere. But, young woman, run for your life."

"I shall stay," said Florinda, "for your son might know how I can reach the Green Moss Prince. Please hide me."

So, the Wind's mother hid her in a big closet.

A few minutes later, the Wind approached, blowing furiously, howling and breaking everything on his passage. He finally began to bang wildly on the door, which the old woman hastened to open.

"O," he began, "what a world and what a day! But . . . what does this mean? I smell human flesh and blood. . . ."

"O, son, be quiet, there is no human being here. It is true that a few hours ago a girl dropped by, but ran away as soon as she found out that this was the Wind's home. Now sit down and eat your supper."

During the meal, the old woman told the Wind of the girl's plight.

"Why did you not let her stay?" he asked.

"If you would talk to her, you can do it immediately." And the woman went out for the girl.

But the Wind could not tell the trembling Florinda where she could find her prince, nor the Kingdom of the Green Moss.

She spent the night in the house, and the following morning, as he was getting ready to leave, the Wind handed her something and advised:

> "It may be of assistance to you some day.
> Good luck."

Florinda resumed her tiresome journey. She walked and walked. Her second pair of iron shoes was worn

out. One day she saw a small white house on the top of a hill. She decided to knock. A pleasant little woman, wearing a white cap, came to the door. To Florinda's request to stay overnight, frightened, she answered:

> *"It is impossible, my child. The Moon, my daughter, is very whimsical. Should she be in one of her moods tonight she will kill you."*

"Tell me, please, do you know where the Kingdom of the Green Moss is?"

"Never heard of it," replied the pleasant little woman. "My daughter might know. But I really do not think it will be wise for you to stay."

Spurred on by her desire, Florinda persuaded the old woman to hide her.

The Moon was in a bad temper. When she came in, she cried that she smelled human flesh and blood, but the smiling old lady soothed her and told her that actually a girl had called, but had scampered away upon being told that the house was the Moon's home.

"She was seeking the Kingdom of the Green Moss," added the woman.

"Why did you chase her away?" inquired the Moon.

"Would you actually like to talk to her?" asked the mother.

The Moon said "Yes." Her mother produced a shaking Florinda, doomed once more to disappointment; for the Moon, who goes everywhere, had never heard of the Kingdom of the Green Moss. The Moon, however, likes to dream, and takes an interest in lovers. So when, on the following morning, Florinda was getting ready to leave, she made her a present and added:

"It may be of help to you some day."

And so the poor girl started once more on her dreary journey. She walked and walked, until her third pair of iron shoes was nearly worn out. One evening, she saw the outlines of a bright house on the dark background of the falling night. She approached it and knocked on the door.

A large woman peered at her. Florinda begged to be allowed to stay for the night.

"It is evident you do not know that this is the dwelling of the Sun, the King of Day. My son could never bear the presence of a mortal under his roof."

Finally persuaded by Florinda's entreaties and by the story of her woes, she consented to hide her.

All of a sudden the house was filled with a strange light that dazzled and burnt. The Sun had come in. The moment after, he was roaring:

"I smell human flesh and blood."

"Right, son," interposed the old lady. "A girl called here, but left as soon as she found out that this was your dwelling."

As the Sun eagerly devoured his supper, the mother inquired whether he knew where the Kingdom of the Green Moss was.

"Yes, I do, but why do you ask me?"

When he understood the plight of the girl, he felt sorry and expressed his disappointment at not being able to help her.

"If that is so," commented the old woman, "it still is time." And she brought Florinda into the presence of the Sun.

"I was today in the Kingdom of the Green Moss," he said. "Everybody is making merry there, for three days hence their king will be married."

"O, heavens!" said the girl, "I shall not have time to get there."

"I shall carry you on my rays," promised the Sun.

Before dawn, the following day, the Sun started on his daily journey, bearing Florinda on his rays.

After a few moments, he asked her to alight, and after presenting a wonderful gift to her, he advised her to act quickly, and was gone.

Florinda looked around. She was in a beautiful city, all decorated with flags and flowers. So her prince was getting married? She sat down on a lawn to think. Her eyes rested on the present given her by the Wind. It was a small, golden spinning wheel that spun threads of gold.

Florinda sprang to her feet and walked away, inquiring for the king's palace. She finally found it.

"That window up there," a gossiping woman told her, "is the chamber of the princess, of the one who will be our queen within three days." Florinda sat directly under that window, and, taking out the golden spinning wheel, she set it to work.

She did not have long to wait until one of the princess's chambermaids peered out of the window and saw what was going on.

"How wonderful," she exclaimed, and sent word to the princess. The latter, accompanied by her ladies-in-waiting, leaned out of the window. One of the maids was dispatched to buy the spinning wheel from Florinda.

"I shall not part with it for any sum of money," declared the owner.

"What would you have, then?" eagerly asked the maid.

"Tell your mistress that if she allows me to spend a night in the chamber adjoining the king's rooms, she may have my spinning wheel."

The princess laughed at the queer idea and ordered that she be admitted into the palace.

When everything was quiet in the palace, Florinda began to sob aloud in her chamber.

"Ungrateful green parrot," she wailed, "you pretended to believe that I had tried to hurt you, but in your heart you well knew that I was innocent." And in this strain she went on for a long time.

Nobody stirred in the adjoining room. Nothing happened.

The following day, Florinda sat down again under the same palace window, displaying a marvelous golden lace cushion, the gift of the Moon. It worked by itself, making the most exquisite, cobweb-like gold lace.

It was not long before the same maid saw her again, and not long before she parted with the marvelous object at the same price set before.

Nothing unusual happened at night, and the girl's cries seemed to pass unheeded. Very early in the morning, however, as she was leaving her room, the king's chamberlain approached her and remarked:

> *"You must keep quiet at night. But for the*
> *potion the king takes in order to be able to*

sleep, he would be disturbed by your wailing and wild words about, of all things, a green parrot."

"Sir," burst out the poor girl, "do not give the king that potion tonight, and I shall handsomely reward you."

Going out, Florinda laid her hands on her last precious possession, the gift of the Sun. It consisted of a golden hen and six little golden chicks, every one thoroughly alive and perfectly beautiful. It certainly made a spectacle when the mother hen began to peck and her little ones to run around and peep. The princess was highly pleased, and Florinda's strange request was once more complied with.

When all the noises subsided in the palace, Florinda started her wailing once more.

Turning in bed, the prince asked the chamberlain:

"What does this mean?"

"Your Majesty, for some unknown reason, a little waif has been spending the nights in the adjoining chamber, and seemingly, in her leisure hours, she indulges in wail-like songs about a green parrot."

"Chamberlain," His Majesty uttered excitedly, "dress me at once."

The prince of the Kingdom of the Green Moss went into Florinda's chamber, and after an explanation, the lovers were reconciled.

The following day, instead of going to the altar, the foreign princess was dispatched to her father's kingdom, while the beauteous Florinda, radiant with goodness, beauty, and love, was made the queen of a lovely country, and, which she esteemed more, of the heart of its prince.

READING FOR UNDERSTANDING

1. Why did the widow take a special interest in Florinda? What was her plan?
2. What did the youngest daughter find out about Florinda?
3. We can assume there was something special about the tea that Florinda served the sisters. What do you think it was?
4. The prince was harsh to Florinda and gave her a difficult task to accomplish. Why? Was it necessary to the story?
5. How did the Wind, the Moon, and the Sun change in their reactions to Florinda? Why do you think this was?
6. Do you think that Florinda and the prince "lived happily ever after"? Why or why not?

RESPONDING TO THE STORY

This story never gave an explanation for why the prince took the form of a parrot. Use your imagination to come up with a reason for his transformation.

REVIEWING VOCABULARY

Match each word on the left with the correct definition on the right.

1. dullard
2. entrusted
3. swarthy
4. gaunt
5. abode
6. plight
7. whimsical
8. entreaties
9. adjoining
10. esteemed

a. home; residence
b. stupid person
c. unpredictable
d. strong requests
e. given a duty
f. having a dark complexion
g. serious situation
h. thought of with high regard
i. side by side
j. thin and bony

THINKING CRITICALLY

1. This folktale states quite clearly how beautiful and virtuous Florinda was, but she had many other traits as well. Describe what she was like, as shown by her behavior in the story.

2. The youngest daughter of the widow was described as ugly and one-eyed. Why do you think the storyteller portrayed her this way? Did her outward appearance reflect her inner nature? Why might folktales simplify characters in this way?

3. When Florinda was next to the prince's room, she wailed, "You pretended to believe that I tried to hurt you, but in your heart you well knew that I was innocent." Did this statement surprise you after all that Florinda had gone through to get to the kingdom? Why did she say it?

4. Florinda's love was put to a very severe test. What did you find to be the most difficult part of her test? Describe some thoughts that Florinda might have had that were not mentioned in the story.

DON'T MAKE A BARGAIN WITH A FOX
a folktale from Argentina
By M.A. Jagendorf and R.S. Boggs

Many folktales use animals to represent the ways that humans behave. Sometimes it is easier to describe our failings—or the abilities of others—by having animals take human roles. "Brave as a lion." "Wise as an owl." "Sly as a fox." These are just a few of the many expressions used to describe human behavior by using particular animals who seem to show human qualities.

The fox appears in stories from many cultures. There are good reasons for this. The fox can be found around farms, in forests, in deserts, even on the edges of cities. It is very difficult to capture. Perhaps this is why many cultures portray the fox as smart and sly. For example, one of Aesop's fables tells of the fox who was so clever that he could talk a hungry raven out of his dinner.

In the following folktale, set on the pampas (grassy plains) of Argentina, the fox makes a bargain with two little rodents, called viscachas. *As the title of the story suggests, other animals should be very careful when dealing with a fox—just as people should be careful when dealing with a "sharp" character.*

VOCABULARY WORDS

scampering (SKAM-puhr-ihng) running quickly
❖ The rabbits were *scampering* all over the backyard.

stubble (STUB-uhl) short stumps of grain left in the ground
❖ After the harvest, only *stubble* was left in the field.

blotches (BLAH-chihz) large spots or stains
❖ Because of the cold weather, her dark face had red *blotches*.

ragged (RAG-ihd) torn and uneven
❖ The edge of the paper was *ragged*.

keen (KEEN) sharp; shrewd
❖ She was well known for her *keen* mind.

loping (LOH-pihng) moving easily with a long stride
❖ The dog was *loping* happily through the meadow.

KEY WORDS

pampas (PAHM-pahs) treeless plains in South America
❖ The ostrich lives on the *pampas*.

compadres (kohm-PAH-drays) Spanish word for friends
❖ The Mexican farmer waved to his *compadres*.

**S**ome time back, a long time ago, two *viscachas*—rodent animals, about the size of a hare—lived together in the brush of the Argentine pampas. They were good friends, and they were always together. One day they were scampering along over the stubble and the grass, smelling this and smelling that, and now and then stopping to do a little gnawing. It was pleasant for them to live on the great pampas of Argentina.

Suddenly they saw two red blotches. They ran up to them carefully—you never can tell what you'll meet on the pampas. They went up to those red blotches and sniffed. They were two pieces of a ragged red blanket someone had left, either forgotten or thrown away.

"This is a valuable treasure," said one.

"Some Indian must have forgotten it and left it here. Or maybe he didn't know he dropped it," said the other.

"In any case, we've found it and it's ours," said the first.

"Yes, it's ours. What shall we do with it?"

"Well, I know. Let's use it for a blanket. We can cover ourselves with it when it's cold."

"That's a good idea. But, look, I'm lying on one piece all stretched out, and it's too small."

"Yes, it is too small, but we can sew the two pieces together."

"Yes, we could do that, but where can we find a needle and some thread?"

"That's a thought. I haven't any, and you haven't either."

"What shall we do?"

"I don't know."

They sat looking at each other, wiggling their sharp little noses up and down.

Just then, Señor Fox came along. He had a long nose and a long tail, and a keen brain in his head besides.

"*Buenos días*, good day, my good friends," he said. "You look worried. Is anything wrong?"

"Yes!" they both said at once. "We need a needle and some thread to sew together these two pieces of our fine new blanket."

"What will you do with it after you have sewed it?"

"We'll cover ourselves with it on cold nights," they both answered. "It will keep us warm."

"I'll give you a needle and some thread if you'll let me share your fine blanket."

"That we will. Just give us the needle and thread."

Señor Fox gave them the needle and thread, and they went to work. In a short time the two pieces were sewed together.

"You have done a fine piece of work," said Señor Fox. "Now give me back my needle. I'll see you tonight." Then he went away.

The little *viscachas* ran around and picked up bits of

food here and there. Night came, and the cold wind began to blow all over the pampas.

"This is the time of year when our blanket will feel good," they said, and they were very pleased with themselves.

Señor Fox came loping along. "Good evening, my good little friends," he said.

"Good evening, *buenas noches*, Señor Fox."

"It's a cold night, *compadres*."

"Yes, it is a cold night, Señor Fox."

"But *we* won't be cold, *compadres*. You have that fine blanket, for which I lent you my needle and thread. If it weren't for me, you wouldn't have a blanket at all, so I have as much right to it as you do."

"Yes, that's true, Señor Fox."

"Now, let's see," Señor Fox said, and scratched his head. "Let's see, I gave you the needle and I gave you the thread, and you used my thread to sew it down the middle, so the middle is really my part."

"That sounds right, Señor Fox."

"Then the right thing is for me to lie under the middle part, which is my part, and for you two to be on the sides, which are your parts."

"That sounds right, Señor Fox."

So Señor Fox lay down on the ground, and the two *viscachas* put the middle of the blanket over him. Then they lay down, one on each side of him.

Now, you know that Señor Fox is large and wide, so the blanket covered him, but there was little left to cover the two poor *viscachas* lying on either side. Each one had only one edge of the blanket, which barely reached halfway across his body, leaving the other half out in the cold wind. And that's the way they had to lie, shivering all night long.

So, you see that you can never strike a bargain with a fox. He'll get the best of you every time.

READING FOR UNDERSTANDING

The following paragraph summarizes the folktale. Decide which of the words below the paragraph best fits in each blank. Some words may be used more than once. Write your answers on a separate sheet of paper.

A long time ago, on the **(1)**_____ pampas, two **(2)**_____ were good **(3)**_____ and were always together. One day, they found two pieces of a **(4)**_____ that someone had **(5)**_____ or thrown away. They decided to use the pieces as a **(6)**_____, but realized that the pieces were too **(7)**_____. They wanted to **(8)**_____ the pieces together, but they needed a **(9)**_____ and some **(10)**_____. When the fox came along and heard their story, he offered to give them a **(11)**_____ and some **(12)**_____ if they would agree to share the **(13)**_____. They accepted his offer and sewed the two pieces together. Later that cold night, the fox came back and asked to **(14)**_____ the **(15)**_____. He convinced them that he should lie under the **(16)**_____ part, so the two **(17)**_____ lay down on either **(18)**_____ of him. Because the fox was so big, the *viscachas* were cold all night long.

Words: *Argentine, blanket, forgotten, friends, middle, needle, sew, share, side, small, thread,* viscachas

RESPONDING TO THE STORY

Imagine that the case of the blanket is being tried in court. Come up with an argument for why the fox *was* or *was not* entitled to use the middle of the blanket. Prepare your case by writing down reasons for your position, and defend it.

REVIEWING VOCABULARY

Match each word on the left with the correct definition on the right.

1. scampering
2. stubble
3. blotches
4. ragged
5. keen
6. loping

a. moving easily with a long stride
b. torn and uneven
c. running quickly
d. sharp; shrewd
e. short stumps of grain left in the ground
f. large spots or stains

THINKING CRITICALLY

1. There is a saying that goes: "You can't argue with logic." Does this folktale support that statement? Tell why it does or does not.
2. Describe the fox in terms of his appearance, speech, and behavior. Is his portrayal similar to that in other tales you have read? Can you name other tales with a fox, either as the main character or a secondary character, and tell the story?
3. This story seems to suggest that it's possible to be "too nice for your own good." Give evidence from the story. Do you agree or disagree?
4. Ask students what elements of folktales are demonstrated in the story.

THE TREE OF LIFE
a story of the Carib people
Retold by Richard Alan Young and Judy Dockrey Young

In ancient times, people invented stories in order to explain things in nature. Today, such stories are known as creation myths.

"The Tree of Life" is an example of a creation myth. It was told by generation after generation of Native American Caribs. This group of people lived on the Windward Islands in the Caribbean Sea. Members of this group were also found in the Amazon River Valley of northeastern South America.

At the heart of this myth is the human wonder at the variety and amount of food that nature provides. As you read, think about the roles of the animal characters. Which human traits do they personify, or represent?

VOCABULARY WORDS

sleek (SLEEK) well-fed or well-groomed
❖ With good care, the skinny kitten became a *sleek* cat.

rodent (ROHD-uhnt) one of a group of animals with large front teeth used for chewing
❖ One type of *rodent* is a squirrel.

council (KOWN-suhl) group called together to discuss something
❖ The students formed a *council* to discuss the library.

rustling (RUS-lihng) making soft sounds
❖ We heard leaves *rustling* in the breeze.

sternly (STERN-lee) in a serious and strict manner
❖ She *sternly* told her son to go up to his room.

KEY WORDS

cassava (kuh-SAH-vuh) tropical American plants with edible roots of the tropics
❖ The Caribs later planted *cassava* roots.

agouti (ah-GOO-tee) a large forest rodent
❖ The *agouti* found a place where there was food.

cane (KAYN) strips stems of certain plants, such as bamboo
❖ The Caribs had never seen *cane* strips before.

calabash (KAL-uh-bash) large gourd-like fruit from a tropical tree of the same name
❖ She found a *calabash* on the ground.

gourd (GOHRD) dried, hollowed-out shell of certain fruits
❖ He poured water into the *gourd*.

Makunaima (mah-koo-NY-mah) creator god
❖ The chiefs called on *Makunaima* on important days.

**I**n the beginning of the Forest World, the Carib people had very little to eat. (They had not yet learned to plant cassava roots.) The animals and birds also had very little to eat. Everyone was hungry.

But one little animal, the agouti, a large forest rodent, seemed sleek and fat and healthy. He went out every morning, far away into the forest. When he came back in the evening he seemed to have eaten. He dropped banana skins, cane strips, and other things the people and animals had never seen.

The people and animals called a council and spoke to each other. They decided that the little agouti must have found a place where there was food to eat.

They decided to send one animal to follow the agouti when he went out the next morning, to see where he went. The animal could then come back and tell the rest of them. The first day, they sent the snake.

The snake waited for the agouti to pass on his morning journey. Then he followed the little rodent a long, long way into the forest. The snake saw the agouti stop and look back to see if anyone was following him. The snake became afraid that he had been seen or heard rustling among the leaves. He stayed behind, and the agouti went on.

The snake had nothing to report. Yet the agouti came back looking well-fed again that evening.

The next morning the people and animals selected the woodpecker to fly above the forest floor and watch the agouti from above. The agouti looked around and did not see or hear anything following him on the ground. But the woodpecker saw some bugs in the bark of a tall tree. He could not help but peck on the bark a little bit to get some of the bugs to eat.

The agouti heard the woodpecker and suspected he was being followed, so he picked up some bitter weeds and pretended to chew them as if they were what he ate.

The woodpecker reported back to the people and animals. They tasted the bitter weeds and knew they had been fooled.

The next day the people and the animals sent the rat to follow the agouti. Brother rat is the most sneaky and quiet of all the animals. He has to hide from people and meat-eaters all the time, and he can move more quietly than anyone.

The agouti never knew the rat was following him. He stopped and looked all around and listened high and low, and when he could not hear or see anyone following him, he went to his secret place.

Brother rat followed.

The agouti went to the tallest tree in the forest. He gathered all manner of fruit from the ground underneath the tree. It was a most wonderful tree! Every fruit grew on its branches: bananas, plums, mangos, papayas. Every good root grew at the foot of the tree: cassava, yucca, yams. Every good berry and bean grew under its leaves, and every good grass and grain grew from its bark.

As soon as the agouti had eaten his fill, he wiped his face with his paws and went away.

The rat came back and told the people and the animals what he had seen. They all went back to the tree, led by the rat.

By the time they reached the tree, many ripe fruits and other good things had fallen to the ground. They picked these up and ate them. After everyone was full, they talked about how to get more fruits and food down. No one could climb the tree. It was too big and the bark was too smooth.

After much talking, they decided to cut the tree down so they could reach all the fruit and berries and food growing on it, and dig up all its good roots to eat.

The people and the animals went and got stone axes

and began to cut. They cut for ten days, but the tree would not fall. They cut for another ten days, and still the tree would not fall. By now they were very hungry again, and very thirsty.

The people got calabash gourds off the lower parts of the tree and cut them open to make water-carriers. Each animal was given a gourd to carry water in, so everyone would have something to drink while they worked.

But the agouti, who had come upon them cutting the tree on the second day, was sternly punished for being so greedy and keeping the tree to himself. Everyone scolded him, especially the monkey, who scolds so much even today.

When all the animals were given gourds to carry water in, they gave the agouti a basket woven of grass so he couldn't get much water, as a punishment.

After ten more days of cutting, the tree fell at last.

The people took away as their share what they plant

today: cassava, cane, yams, bananas, potatoes, pumpkins and watermelons. The animals took what they wanted: the birds took seeds and the rodents took grains. Some of the others wanted green leaves, and so on.

The agouti was just getting back from the river, carrying his grass basket without much water left in it. When he got back, only one kind of fruit was left. No one had taken the plums, so they became the food of the agouti.

This was the story about the Tree of Life, sent by Makunaima to feed his people and his animals, and about how the little agouti led the people and the animals to the Tree of Life.

READING FOR UNDERSTANDING

1. In the beginning of the Forest World, **(a)** the Carib people had little to eat **(b)** the animals and birds ate everything **(c)** there was plenty of food for everyone.

2. The Caribs thought that the agouti was eating well because he **(a)** was able to describe many rare foods **(b)** dropped pieces of food that no one had ever seen **(c)** bragged about eating.

3. The agouti tried to avoid being followed by **(a)** not going to the tree **(b)** leaving the forest for good **(c)** playing a trick on the woodpecker.

4. After the tree was cut down, the people gained an advantage over the animals because they **(a)** could eat the animals **(b)** took the best food **(c)** grew their own food.

5. The rat may have been chosen to follow the agouti because he **(a)** could go for days without food **(b)** was used to a life of hiding and being sneaky **(c)** was so mean.

RESPONDING TO THE STORY

1. Though the agouti led the people and animals to the Tree of Life, they decided to punish him. Write a paragraph telling why the agouti was punished. Do you think it was a just punishment? Why or why not?

2. Do you think that the people and animals should have cut down the tree? Why or why not? Explain your answer.

3. Which part of this myth stood out or caused a strong reaction as you read? Identify the part, and tell why you think it affected you as it did.

REVIEWING VOCABULARY

The following sentences are based on the myth. Decide which of the words following the sentences best fits each blank. Write your answers on a separate sheet of paper.

1. The Caribs told how it was the agouti, a healthy _____, who led them to the Tree of Life.
2. A _____ of people and animals met to discuss why he was so _____ and healthy.
3. When the snake tried to follow, he thought he could be heard _____ through the leaves.
4. When the Tree of Life was found, the greedy animal was _____ punished and scolded, especially by the monkeys.

Words: *council, rustling, sternly, rodent, sleek*

THINKING CRITICALLY ABOUT CULTURE

1. One aspect of folktales is the use of the number three, as in three kings or three wishes. Find an example of the use of the number three in this myth. What effect does it create?
2. The myth tells us that "the people and animals called a council and spoke to each other." What does this tell you about the relationship long ago between the people and animals?
3. In myths, animals often have human traits. Support this statement with descriptions of the behavior of the agouti, the woodpecker, and the rat.

HOW THE ALLIGATOR GOT HIS SCALES
a tale from the Amazon
By Elsie Spicer Fields

The creation myth you are about to read comes from the Amazon. This area surrounding the mighty Amazon River runs thousands of miles through the jungles of South America. It is a land of lush beauty and home to many creatures.

Much of this region, especially the rainforests, has been destroyed by careless mining, farming, and industry. Scientists have described the terrible effects that the destruction of the rainforests has on the balance of nature.

People in ancient times had no scientific knowledge about the world around them. They did understand, though, its importance and the need to honor and protect it.

Ancient people were wise enough to see how all life is strongly connected. Their need to make sense of the world was as strong as our scientific curiosity. Out of this need came explanations about why animals look and behave the way they do. No one questions why the alligator has big teeth, but why he has scales needs some explanation.

VOCABULARY WORDS

iridescent (ihr-uh-DEH-suhnt) showing changes in color when seen from various angles
❖ The fabric of her dress was *iridescent*.

dwelt (DWEHLT) lived in a place
❖ The old man *dwelt* in the cabin until he died.

gadabouts (GAD-uh-bowts) those who go around looking for fun
❖ The *gadabouts* had a great time going to many parties.

scheme (SKEEM) plan or plot
❖ The robbers had a *scheme* for robbing the bank.

taunting (TAWN-tihng) insulting
❖ The boys were *taunting* the child who couldn't swim.

meekly (MEEK-lee) weakly; humbly
❖ She meekly *apologized* for keeping us waiting.

borne (BAWRN) produced
❖ The alligator had *borne* scales to show where he was beaten.

Now Rairu ruled the world with law and order. Everything had its appointed place. The sun and the moon, which had been set in the sky, had their own paths, and when they were not in use, they were kept in big pots with the lids tightly fastened on. Every bright star which shone in the violet sky at night had its own appointed place. In the earth, each beast had its own duties to perform, and each flower had its own color and its own sweet perfume. In the sea, even the fishes had their own paths, and the same was true in the rivers and lakes. Every little fish had its own coat of lovely iridescent colors, blue and silver and mauve and gold and pink and brown and black and gray and white.

It so happened that in a certain little river, the pretty rose and silver fishes which dwelt there would not stay at home.

"What am I going to do with you to keep you from being such silly little gadabouts?" asked Rairu one day, when he visited them. "I have scolded and scolded you until I am tired!"

"We do not know," answered the little rose and silver fishes. "We are very sorry when you scold us. We always promise you that we'll do better next time."

"I know you do that," answered the great Rairu very sadly. "But as soon as my back is turned, you do not seem to remember your promises at all. I'll try you just once more. This time, if you do not stay where you belong, I shall think up some new scheme to fix you. Wait and see!"

And so Rairu went away to visit other lakes and rivers and gardens. Soon, however, he returned to the river where he had left the little rose and silver fishes, to see if they were obeying him. Not a single one of them could he find there.

"Now I am going to fix you there so you cannot get

out!" thundered he, when he once more had collected them in their appointed place. "You know what I told you the last time I was here."

"Yes, we know," answered the little fishes sadly. "And we are very sorry that we are such gadabouts!"

"I am tired of hearing that story!" cried Rairu. "This is going to be a different one!"

Then Rairu set to work at building a great dam in the river. He called all the beasts to come and help him. There was none of them so good at building as was the beaver, and so he has remained a builder even until now.

When at last the fine dam was completed, Rairu said to the pretty little fishes, "Now see if you are not entirely cured of being such silly little gadabouts!"

So Rairu went away over the hills and mountains and through the forests and jungles to visit other parts of the great beautiful world which he so dearly loved. After a long time, he came back to visit the little rose and silver fishes he had left safely fastened in their own river by means of the strong dam. He called them and he called them, but there was no answer. The dam was broken, and they all had run away.

"What can be the cause of this?" asked Rairu in anger. "The little fishes cannot be to blame for breaking the dam. They are silly, foolish little things, it is true, but somebody else has broken the dam."

Rairu at last called together all the rose and silver fishes which had run away and safely herded them back into their own place. Then he called together the beasts to repair the dam. That was the time he heard the alligator boasting.

"Very smart indeed you think yourselves," he was boasting. "But you cannot build a dam which will be strong enough to keep me from breaking it if I wish."

"So you are the one who broke my fine dam and let the little fishes swim away again!" cried the angry Rairu when he had heard these taunting words. "I shall arrange things with you so you will not want to break my dam again!"

With these words, the mighty Rairu seized a great tree as a club and beat the alligator so that he was all covered with scales on his back and sides.

"Now will you break my dam and let my little fishes swim away from their appointed place?" thundered the great voice of Rairu.

"No," replied the alligator very meekly. "I will never break your dam again."

To this very day, the alligator has borne scales along his back and his sides where he was beaten by the club of the mighty Rairu.

READING FOR UNDERSTANDING

1. Describe how Rairu ruled the world.
2. Why do you think Rairu was so interested in the rose and silver fishes?
3. How did the rose and silver fishes misbehave?
4. How did Rairu's reaction to the fishes change over time?
5. How does the building of the dam explain another fact of nature?
6. Who interfered with Rairu's plan, and how?
7. In what way were the gadabouts like little children?
8. How did the alligator get his scales? Why?
9. Why do you think it was important to Rairu that everything be in order?

RESPONDING TO THE STORY

The beginning of the myth describes a very ordered universe. Everything has its place and purpose. Do you agree that this is so, or do you disagree? Explain your thinking with examples.

REVIEWING VOCABULARY

1. An *iridescent* shirt appears to have many **(a)** stripes **(b)** colors **(c)** wrinkles.
2. Sara *dwelt* in Chicago. This means she **(a)** visited there **(b)** worked there **(c)** lived there.
3. *Gadabouts* would most likely enjoy **(a)** reading quietly **(b)** going to parties **(c)** seeing a movie.
4. Who would most likely have a *scheme?* **(a)** a burglar **(b)** a baby **(c)** a tree
5. You would most likely hear *taunting* remarks **(a)** in a playground **(b)** at a library **(c)** in a hospital.
6. Someone who speaks *meekly* is **(a)** happy **(b)** shy **(c)** angry.

7. If the tree had *borne* fruit, it had **(a)** sour fruit **(b)** some fruit **(c)** no fruit.

THINKING CRITICALLY

1. According to the story, how is everything in the universe kept in order? Give evidence from the myth.

2. Both the fishes and the alligator upset Rairu, but he treated them differently. Why? Do you agree with his reactions?

3. Do you think Rairu's punishment of the alligator was too harsh? Why or why not?

4. What does Rairu's behavior toward the alligator tell you about how the people of the Amazon view nature and the world around them?

5. Do you think this would be a good story to use in a discussion about the rainforests? Why or why not?

ACKNOWLEDGMENTS

Atheneum Books for Young Readers, an imprint of Simon & Schuster Children's Publishing Division, for Frank Henius, "The Baker's Neighbor" and "The Green Moss Prince" from *Stories from the Americas* translated by Frank Henius. Copyright © 1944, **Charles Scribners Sons,** renewed 1972 Gertrude Henius and Leo Politi. **August House, Inc.,** for Richard Alan Young with Judy Dockrey Young, "The Tree of Life" from *Stories from the Days of Christopher Columbus,* collected and retold by Richard Alan Young with Judy Dockrey Young. Copyright © 1992. **Children's Book Press,** for Harriet Rohmer and Jesus Guerrero Rea, "Atariba and Niguayona, a Story from the Taino People of Puerto Rico," adapted by Harriet Rohmer and Jesus Guerrero Rea. Copyright 1988. **Dial Books for Young Readers, a division of Penguin Books USA Inc.,** for Julius Lester, "The Cradle Didn't Rock" from *The Tales of Uncle Remus by Julius Lester.* Copyright 1987. **Doubleday, a division of Bantam Doubleday Dell Publishing Group, Inc.,** for James D. Sexton, "The Story of the Lazy Man Who Got to Be King of a Town" from *Mayan Folktales* by James D. Sexton. Copyright © 1992 by James D. Sexton. **Greenwillow Books/William Morrow & Company, Inc.,** for Dorothy de Wit, "Ojeeg, the Hunter, and the Ice Man" from *The Talking Stone,* edited by Dorothy de Wit. Reprinted by permission of Adriaan de Wit for the estate of Dorothy de Wit. Copyright 1979. **HarperCollins Publishers,** for I.G. Edmonds, "Señor Coyote and the Tricked Trickster" from *Trickster Tales* by I. G. Edmonds. Copyright 1966 by I. G. Edmonds. **Linnet Books,** for Anita Brenner, "The Bow, the Deer, and the Talking Bird" from *The Boy Who Could Do Anything and Other Mexican Folk Tales* by Anita Brenner. Copyright 1992, Susannah Glusker. **Macmillan Books for Young Readers, an imprint of Simon and Schuster Children's Publishing Division,** for Paul Yee, "Ginger for the Heart," from *Tales from the Gold Mountain* by Paul Yee. Text copyright © 1989 Paul Yee. Also for Anne Pellowski, "Why Corn Has Silky White Hair,", from *Hidden Stories in Plants* by Anne Pellowski. Text copyright © 1990 Anne Pellowski. **Mariposa Publishing,** for Joe Hayes, "The Day It Snowed Tortillas" from *Tales from Spanish New Mexico* retold by Joe Hayes. Copyright 1982. **Morrow Junior Books, a division of William Morrow & Company, Inc.,** for John Bierhorst, "Lord Sun's Bride" from *The Monkey's Haircut* by John Bierhorst. Copyright © 1986 by John Bierhorst. Penguin USA, for Pura Belpré, "Pedro Animala and the Carrao Bird" by Pura Belpré from *Folktales from Around the World, Tales of Trickery.* Copyright 1990. **University of Hawaii Press** for Vivian L. Thompson, "A Strange Sled Race" from *Hawaiian Myths of Earth, Sea, and Sky* by Vivian L. Thompson. Copyright 1966. **Vanguard Press, a division of Random House, Inc.,** for M.A. Jagendorf and R.S. Boggs, "Don't Make a Bargain with a Fox" from *The King of the Mountains: A Treasury of Latin American Folkstories* by M. A. Jagendorf and R. S. Boggs. Copyright © 1960 by M. A. Jagendorf and R. S. Boggs. Copyright renewed 1988 by Andre Jagendorf, Merna Alpert and R. S. Boggs. **Walker Books Ltd. (UK) and Candlewick Press (U.S.),** for Michael Rosen, "The Little Green Frog" from *South and North, East and West,* edited by Michael Rosen. Text copyright © 1992 by Michael Rosen. **Diane Wolkstein,** for "A Very Happy Donkey," from *The Magic Orange Tree.* Copyright 1978 by Diane Wolkstein.

Globe Fearon has made a reasonable and concerted effort to contact the writers and/or owners of "How Thunder and Lightning Came to Be" by Ramona Maher and "How the Alligator Got His Scales" by Elsie Spicer Fields. The publisher eagerly invites any persons with knowledge of the whereabouts of these authors or agents to contact Globe Fearon Publishers to arrange for the customary publishing transactions.